ON ONE
condition

Diane Alberts

Previously released on Entangled's Ever After imprint in February 2012

Entangled Publishing, LLC
2614 South Timberline Road
Suite 109
Fort Collins, CO 80525
Visit our website at www.entangledpublishing.com.

Indulgence is an imprint of Entangled Publishing, LLC.

Edited by Adrien-Luc Sanders
Cover design by Liz Pelletier

Manufactured in the United States of America

First Edition February 2012

To my Mom. For being there to listen, plot, plan, praise, and love. This one's for you.

Chapter One

The moment she rolled over, Johanna regretted last night.

It wasn't just the bright light stabbing through her window and straight into her eyes. It wasn't even the pounding headache that made her fairly certain she'd drunk the entire contents of the bar last night. Hell, it wasn't even that it was Valentine's Day, the entire reason she and her friends had decided to toast the town with a lot of drinking and less dancing—on her part, anyway.

No, it was the bright green eyes and handsome face looking back at her, and the small smile on pulse-poundingly full lips.

Son of a bitch.

"Oh," Johanna said. "Oh, crap."

"Hey there." British accent. Her weakness. "I'm sorry, but I don't remember your name. I'm—"

Raising a hand, she groaned and sat up, pulling the sheet over her chest. Her hip rubbed against something hard and hot, and coarse body hair. *Shoot me. Shoot me now.*

"We probably didn't share names," she responded. "Look. I don't usually do this. Let's skip the uncomfortable bullshit and say goodbye."

His lips quirked. "For someone who doesn't do this a lot, you sure have the 'get the hell out of my apartment' speech figured out."

She stared him down. The withering look that could cow every kindergarten student she'd ever taught had zero effect on him. He only stared back at her, raising a brow.

"Please," she said. Mortification made her curt. "Get out."

He chuckled. "You Americans are quite bossy, you know."

She hid her face in her raised knees. "Yep."

"Don't you know who I am?"

She snorted and rolled her eyes. Typical egotistical male. "Didn't we already cover this?"

She heard a chuckle, followed by the rustle of clothing. Peek. No, don't peek. Don't peek at all. She couldn't. She wasn't that kind of woman. She held her breath and kept her head down until she heard the rasp of a zipper.

When she looked up he was standing at her bedside, offering a business card. "If you ever want to—"

"Nope. Keep your card."

He shook his head. "Happy Valentine's Day."

Her fingers clenched against a pillow. Another word out of his mouth, and she'd throw it at his head. "Yeah. Same to you."

Giving her one last lingering look, he left. She held her breath until she heard the front door click shut. She sucked in a whoosh of air and collapsed back on the bed.

Holy shit.

Who had he been? Whoever he was, he'd been absolutely delicious—and she hoped she never saw him again. She was just *that* girl to him, now. Well, as much as an uptight OCD teacher could ever be *that* girl to anyone.

It figured. The first time she let loose, and she couldn't even remember what she'd done.

A hot shower didn't help, or ease her screaming headache. Hell, neither did the coffee, Motrin, or clean clothing, and by the time Johanna made it to work, she was ready to kill someone. Anyone.

To top it off, Rowling Elementary looked like a nightmare. Red paper hearts everywhere. Streamers. Jaunty love songs on the intercom, adding their shrill notes to the splitting sound of the bells. Would it really be so bad if she set the whole place on fire?

Fuck Valentine's Day.

• • •

The Viscount Damon Haymes plucked the invitation from the chaos of paperwork on his desk and eyed it with dismay.

"Can't I just send them the money?" he asked. "It seems distasteful to purchase a woman for the night. And on Valentine's night, of all nights."

"That's the point." Sprawling on the plush leather couch, Jeff smirked. "All these single women need something to distract them from their melancholy lives on a night when everyone else is getting laid."

"You're such an asshole," Damon said, fighting back

a smile. "An unfortunately correct asshole. I still don't see why I can't donate the money and walk away. Bloody hell, I doubt any of these women will be under the age of sixty."

"You never know. You might get lucky."

"With an octogenarian? God, I loathe these affairs."

"Yep. But it's all for the greater good."

"Says the man who doesn't have to go." Damon muttered under his breath.

"Your father loved these events," Jeff said.

"I'm sure he did. But when Mom died, he just spent the last three years trying to keep busy." Damon's eyes burned at the thought of his parents. Though his father had died a mere six months ago, he still felt the loss of both of them far too strongly. "I guess I might get why, now."

Jeff gave him a sad smile. He cleared his throat and said, "So you're going to make me come out and ask. What happened last night? Who was she? Was she any good?"

Damon fought back a grin. Leave it to Jeff to change the subject at the first sign of emotion. "Don't know, don't know, and you don't need to know."

"Aw, she sucked, huh?" Jeff replied, propping his elbow on his leg. "Didn't know her way around a Brit's body? American men are much different, I've heard. Brits are pale and scrawny. Unlike myself."

Damon glanced down at his own flat stomach and quirked a brow. "Really?"

"Yes. Just look at you. It's sick how scrawny you are." Jeff gave him a onceover. "Girls as hot as that one need real men. Men who know how to treat them between the sheets."

Damon rose to his feet, taking a step closer to Jeff. He towered over his best friend by at least five inches. "You seem to be a bit confused."

Jeff laughed and clapped his shoulder.

"So, what happened?"

"She had no clue who I was," Damon said.

"Yeah, right," Jeff scoffed. "A good actress, you mean?"

"No." Damon glared. "She woke up, saw me, and told me to get the hell out. Wouldn't even tell me her bloody name."

Jeff blinked—and burst into hysterical laughter. "Holy shit," he managed. "She ki—she kicked you out?"

Damon clenched his fists, shoulders stiff. Growling, he punched Jeff's shoulder. "If you don't knock it off…"

Wheezing, Jeff collapsed into a chair and rubbed his eyes. "I have to meet her. Take me to her."

Damon rolled his eyes. "Really, why do I bother with you? She didn't give me her bloody name. She barely said one word to me aside from 'get out.' I doubt I'll see her again."

"It's a shame. It's not often you get to be normal. You can't go to the crapper without someone panting after you."

Damon shrugged, clenching his jaw. The woman had intrigued him in more ways than one, and it irked him she'd refused to even think about seeing him again. What had he done to make her reject him so harshly? They'd had a mutually satisfying night of sex—and he knew she had enjoyed herself, thank you—so why had she felt the need to get rid of him so fast?

He forced a smile. "No big deal. We had fun. It's over. I'm sure I'll find another girl soon enough."

After all, they loved to throw themselves at him.

Jeff gnawed at his lower lip. "I could always do some digging. Find out whose family she's from."

Damon held up his hand. "She's not from a family we'd know. She lived in a tiny apartment on the other side of town. Not a mansion."

"I could still figure out—"

"No," Damon pinched the bridge of his nose. "Let's get ready for this blasted charity event so I can go the hell home. I've got a bloody headache."

"Maybe there'll be a hot teacher there, waiting to be rescued." Jeff said. "I'm so there."

"You're sick."

"I know. Oh, by the way, I finished the paperwork you left on my desk. You're good to go," Jeff said.

Damon smiled. "Good. All those words smashed together were making my head ache."

"It's called a legal document. It's supposed to have words—not pictures." Jeff shook his head.

A knock at the door interrupted them. Damon raised an eyebrow. "Are you expecting someone?"

"Nope."

Shrugging, Damon opened the door. A man, wearing a suit and carrying a briefcase, hovered outside. Sweat lined his upper lip, and his eyes shifted all about the room.

Immediately, Damon knew he didn't like him, but forced a polite smile anyway. "Can I help you, Mr.—?"

"Mr. Johnson. I'm a lawyer from your father's firm. I have to speak to you about his will." Handing Damon a business card, the short lawyer skirted around Damon's substantially larger frame like a scared little mouse.

Damon closed the door, shaking his head in disgust. He didn't recognize the man, but he must be the real thing if he'd made it past security.

"What is it now, Mr. Johnson? Yet another trivial detail that happened to slip through the cracks the ten other times you guys read the will to me?" His damn lawyer was always finding something "important" to inform him of—but why send a lackey this time?

As if he gave a bloody damn.

"Viscount Haymes, this business is—" Johnson cleared his throat, fidgeting with his briefcase. "—very delicate. Perhaps you should sit."

"I'd rather stand," Damon said coldly.

With a snort, Jeff took the papers from Johnson and scanned them. He paled. "No, Damon," he said, sinking into the closest chair. "You really need to sit down for this."

Chapter Two

Johanna gulped another glass of champagne, smoothed her black satin dress, and told herself she wasn't trying to get drunk—again. Why would she want to be drunk, anyway? It wasn't like she was about to whore herself out for a bunch of rich sixty-somethings with more money than personal hygiene. It wasn't like the dress showed off things she'd rather keep hidden behind a pencil skirt and severe blouse. And it wasn't like Tim would be here tonight, smiling that million-dollar smile like she hadn't caught him banging a client. If he even thought about bidding on her tonight, she'd cut off his left nut.

God, she hated these events.

Plunking down the empty glass, she leaned closer to Sara. "Lucy looks like she came to snag a husband."

"Wouldn't you? Rich, old, and he'd only need to reach a hand up her skirt to get off. It's worth the inconvenience."

"Yeah, right. Let the bidding start. Geezer Number One,

or Geezer Number Two?"

"Maybe the one scratching his armpit will swoop in and steal Lucy away," Sara whispered, gesturing to the nearest table. "You never know. He looks pretty feisty."

The man in question closed his eyes and let out a little snore. Sara and Johanna stifled giggles behind their hands. "Oh, God," Johanna mumbled. "This is horrible. I need to get married."

Sara clucked her tongue, shooting Johanna a hurt look. "And leave me here alone? Hell no. We're in this together. Till death do us part."

"I don't recall saying 'I do,'" Johanna whispered.

"And the lovely lady sells for *three* hundred dollars!" the announcer called out, pointing to the uncomfortable-looking woman on stage—like it wasn't obvious who he was talking about. Idiot.

The horrible audio crackled through the dimly lit room. Johanna clapped politely when Lucy descended the stage; the spotlight remained on Lucy the entire way. Johanna tugged the hem of her dress towards her knees, but it still didn't come even close to the general neighborhood of proper.

Johanna muttered, "I can't believe I let you put me in this thing."

"You look hot, and you know it."

"No, I don't. I look cold. And uncomfortable. And my dress is uneven!"

"It's supposed to be, you dolt," Sara said.

"Yeah, whatever," Johanna grumbled.

Sara grinned, motioning up at the stage. "You're next. Smile and look happy."

"I hate you right now."

Taking a deep breath, Johanna chugged Sara's untouched champagne.

"Next up," the announcer called out, "we have the oh-so-popular Johanna Thomas. Last year, Mr. Fortens bid six hundred dollars for her. Who will win the pleasure of her company tonight?"

Plastering on a smile, Johanna stood and worked her way to the stage. She tried to ignore the frantic beating of her heart.

If she had any luck left, she'd make it through the night without having to see—

"Three hundred dollars, for old time's sake."

Yep, she'd be in jail by midnight.

"Three hundred dollars to Mr. Tim Smith. Do I have three-fifty?"

Johanna scowled at Tim.

"Three-fifty, to the gentleman in the back. Do I have four hundred?" A slight pause. Tim raised his hand, and Johanna stomped her foot. "Four hundred to Mr. Smith. Four-fifty?"

Please, God, let someone outbid the bastard. Anyone. Hell, she'd even take the old guy counting his cash. Catching his eye, she smiled; let him think that smile meant he'd get more than forced, polite conversation over dinner, as long as he bid enough to make that tightwad Tim give up.

"Four-fifty to Mr. Davis. Five hundred, anyone?" the announcer called.

Tim grinned, raising his hand.

"Five hundred to Mr. Smith. Do I get five-fifty?"

The old man shrugged, tucking his money away and drinking his beverage. Desperation clawed its way through her like a knife. She'd have to sit beside Tim and not gouge his eyes out.

This would be the worst Valentine's Day ever.

"Going once…twice…"

"I bid two-thousand dollars," a voice called from the side. The British lilt washed over her. She whirled. Green eyes met hers from across the room, his lips pinched tightly. He looked…angry.

Oh, God. Could this night get any worse? Of course the auction would result in the only two men she ever screwed fighting publicly over her. If ever a girl wished the floor would open up and swallow her, it had to be Johanna.

"Look, faggot, you're in America now, and you play by our rules," Tim glowered at her "rescuer." "You have to work your way up to the winning bid."

"Must I?" Her one-night stand turned to the announcer, raising a perfect eyebrow. "I'm willing to double the amount. For the sake of the charity, of course."

"Of course," the announcer echoed, flushing. "We'd be thrilled to accept y-your generosity. Four thousand for the lovely Johanna Thomas, to a Mr.…uh, Mr.…?"

"The Viscount Haymes—but feel free to call me Damon." He bowed. A hush went through the crowd, and people started whispering behind their hands. Damon sighed before turning to Johanna, smiling nonchalantly. "Ready, Johanna?"

Sara caught her eye, and Johanna shrugged. To hell with it. Her legs shook so badly she'd be lucky if she made it off stage without falling and making a complete fool out of herself. The damned spotlight blinding her certainly didn't help matters.

She took Damon's outstretched hand and, with her smile clamped firmly in place, muttered through her teeth, "Are you insane? You just wasted four thousand dollars on me."

Damon swept his eyes over her face and bosom. When she blushed, he grinned and said, "Wasted? I think not."

She allowed him to lead her out of the room and into the banquet hall. "Last night you had me for free, and —"

"Get over here, Johanna."

Tim dug his fingers into her elbow and jerked her away from Damon. She glared at him, yanking free. "Let go."

"You should belong to me. I had you fair and square," Tim growled.

Damon stepped closer, towering over them, his gaze flicking between Johanna and Tim. "Is there a problem here, Johanna?"

"Yes," she hissed. "Tim's an asshat who doesn't understand 'get out and stay out.'"

"Indeed?" Damon examined his nails, then offered Johanna his hand with a cool look. "Shall we, then?"

Johanna slipped her hand into his waiting palm. "Sure."

Tim leaned closer to snarl, "This isn't over yet."

Damon's hand tightened on hers. He spun on his heel and stalked toward Tim. "I suggest you mind your manners in the lady's presence."

"Lady?" Tim scoffed.

Johanna jerked Damon to a stop. "Don't bother. He's not worth the trouble."

With one last lingering look for Tim, Damon brushed past him and escorted Johanna to the private dining area reserved for auction winners. Only when they were out of earshot did he speak. "Who was that insufferable fool?"

Johanna avoided his eyes, scrunching up her nose. "An ex," she admitted reluctantly. "One who won't take no for an answer. Thanks, I guess. Even you're better than enduring another date with him."

"Why, thank you. I think." His lips quirked. "I'm happy to be of service. Shall we sit?"

Damon pulled out a chair at the nearest table, which was covered in rose petals and lit by little tea candles surrounding a crystal decanter. Nearby, an orchestra played soft music.

"Thank you," she murmured. Once he looked settled in, she raised a brow. "So… Viscount, huh?"

A waiter poured their wine, then left when Damon motioned him away. Damon looked so regal that she had no problem imagining him in a castle next to a queen. Next to the goddamned crown jewels. Oh, why had she slept with him? She felt like a…like a *peasant*.

"Yes. Is that going to be a problem?" He took a sip of wine, gazing at her over the rim, his eyes warm and inviting. "It didn't seem to bother you last night."

"I didn't know who or what you were last night." Her cheeks grew warm. She skimmed her fingers along the stem of her wineglass. "So it wasn't an issue."

"You said, 'oh, my Lord' enough last night, I figured you knew all about—"

"Oh my God. Shut up!" she whispered, glancing over her shoulder. Had anyone heard him? God, she hoped not. She looked back at Damon—and locked gazes with his sparkling eyes. "You're horrible."

"What? It's true." He leaned closer. "So, why did you kick me out?"

"I told you." She took a fortifying sip of wine before

continuing, "I don't do the whole one-night stand scene. It's not my style."

"Then why did you?"

"Valentine's Day," she blurted out. She fidgeted with her napkin. When he arched his brows, she continued, "I hate being alone on a day when everyone else is walking around all goofy smiles and flowers. And chocolate. Why do I have to have a boyfriend to get flowers and chocolate? I can go buy them myself."

"Indeed, you could." He grinned. "What does any of this have to do with us?"

"There is no us. Last night, the girls and I went out to celebrate being single—"

"Even though you wish you had someone to buy you things today?"

"I don't. But when everywhere you turn, you see happy smiling couples shoved in your face, the day kind of sucks."

"I see. So, since you hate today, you went out drinking to celebrate hating it. The night before the actual day."

"Yeah. We had to be here tonight, for the auction." She shrugged. "I had a bunch of drinks, got a little sloppy, and in came…you."

Thank god, the waiter. Johanna was saved—or so she thought. Damon's grin widened, and he held up a finger to hold the waiter at bay.

"What happened when I came in?"

"I think you remember," she snapped. She gestured to the waiter. "Shouldn't we order? He looks like he might cry. Or spit in our food. Neither one sounds appealing."

"I'm more interested in learning about you," Damon answered. He met the server's eyes across the room, inclining his head. "But if you insist." When the waiter reached their table, Damon said, "We'll both take the filet mignon and potatoes. Salad with house dressing is fine."

The waiter bustled off and Johanna leveled a look on Damon. "I'm a vegetarian."

"Oh. I'll call him back." Damon began to rise.

Johanna laughed. "I was teasing."

"Hm." He sipped his wine, his eyes not leaving hers. "So...I came in."

"Huh?" Sara was trying to mouth something across the room to Johanna, but she couldn't make out a damn thing. She never could figure out how people did the "read my lips" crap. "What's that?"

"We were discussing last night. We left off where I came into the pub."

"It's not a pub. It's a club. Big difference."

Damon shrugged, biting his lower lip. "If you say so."

"I do." She toyed with her napkin. "You came in, I was drunk, and I did stuff I wouldn't normally do. End of story."

"I was drunk, too. But I'd still like to get to know you better."

He reached out and clasped her shoulder. His warm fingers on her bare skin sent shivers down her spine and made her breaths quicken. She might not recall much of last night, but her body definitely remembered his touch.

"Is that so horrible?" he asked.

"I don't know if I can," she said. "I'm ashamed of my behavior last night. I'm not sure I can look you in the eye. I know a lot of people meet up in bars and have sex, but I don't. It's not me."

"Me neither. So, we go back to the beginning. Get to

know each other. Slowly." He caressed her shoulder one last time before he leaned back. "What do you think?"

She thought she'd like to kiss him. Maybe the taste of him would help her remember last night. "I'll think about the possibility, my lord."

He sighed. "Just call me Damon. When you say 'my lord,' you bring back memories of last night."

"Damon, then. If we're gonna start over, no more talking about last night." She fought back a smile. "Ever."

Groaning, Damon sank back in his chair. "That's tough. I happen to have very fond memories from last night. You expect me to forget them?"

Johanna rolled her eyes. "Do it."

"I'll agree not to mention it. But I won't forget. It's not possible." His gaze drifted over her, caressing her with an intimacy that left her mouth dry. "So, tell me about yourself."

What the hell was she supposed to say to someone like him? "Well, I'm twenty-six. Never been married. No kids. Work in an elementary school as a kindergarten teacher."

"Sounds fascinating." Oddly enough, he sounded sincere. "How long have you been a teacher?"

"Three years now."

"So you've been doing this charity event for three years?"

She blushed. "Yeah. We do the event for the kids. If you're married, you get out of it. But otherwise…"

His eyes darkened. "Married? You get to avoid this if you're married?"

"Um, yes."

"I see. Interesting." His eyes held a far off look, as if he wasn't really paying attention to her. When he simply stared off into the distance for a good minute or so, she craned her neck to see if he saw something she did not.

Following the line of his gaze, she discovered he stared at...the wall. Okay, nothing exciting there. Confused, she cleared her throat and waved a hand in front of his eyes.

"Hello, earth to Damon." His gaze finally returned to her, and she drew back at the determination and intensity in his eyes. Tugging on her uneven dress, she asked, "Uh, are you okay?"

He nodded briskly, rising to his feet. "I have something to ask you. Don't freak out."

"Okay..."

Never dropping his gaze from hers, he lowered himself to one knee. "Johanna, will you marry me?"

Chapter Three

The world stopped. So did everyone around them, and Johanna felt every eye burning into her. She stared at Damon, trembling.

"Stop it," she hissed, and grabbed his elbow. He remained firmly planted on one knee. Her blush crept down, burning her neck, and she bent low. "I'm serious. You may think you're funny, but I don't."

"I'm not kidding. Marry me." His hand rested over his heart.

"Oh, for the love of…" She snatched up her coat and purse and stalked away without a backward glance. How dare he embarrass her like that?

She despised being the center of attention—and in the midst of a fake proposal, no less.

Footsteps thudded behind her, heavy and fast. She knew, without turning, that it was him. She quickened her stride, only to stumble in her damn heels.

"Johanna, wait!" he called out. His voice grew louder as his longer legs overtook her. "You have to listen to me."

She pushed through the doors leading outside. "I don't have to do anything," she managed to gasp out between gulps of air.

"Please," he said. "Give me a chance to explain."

Her hands trembled when she wiped them on her coat. "Are you telling me this isn't some sick joke? You're actually serious?"

"Absolutely."

"Then you're more messed up than I am. And believe me, that's saying a lot." Wrapping her arms around herself, she headed to the bus stop.

"I'll explain everything. Can we go to your place?" he asked as he fell into stride with her. "Or mine?"

She froze, staring at him. How did she manage to always find the crazy men? "You want me to bring you home? For the love of God, you just asked me to marry you—and you don't even know me!"

"Yes." His jaw tightened. "I'll explain everything. But you're shivering, and it's bloody freezing out here. Shall we take your car or mine?"

"I don't have a car," she ground out.

"Then we'll take mine."

"No."

Sliding onto the bus stop bench, she plopped her purse in her lap. He sank down beside her, right in her personal space. She glared at him.

"What? You look cold," he said.

As if. "Isn't it against some sort of noble law to slum around bus stops with the peasants?"

Laughing, he rested his head against the wood, turning his gaze to the stars. "Do you see Orion?"

She eyed him, then glanced up. "Yes. He's pretty much the only one I can ever find."

"It's the belt. Makes him easy to see, since the stars all line up perfectly." He sighed. "If only life were so easy to sort out."

She squinted at the stars. The sky was so clear, the stars so bright. She watched him from the corner of her eye as she searched the sky.

"I know the little dipper is up there somewhere, but I can never find it."

"It's there," he murmured, moving closer. He rested his head beside hers. Tingles shot up her spine until her head swam. "Hm," he said. "It's at ten o'clock, from your viewpoint."

She gave a small shake of her head. They all just looked like globs of stars to her. "I still don't see it."

"Look for the little box." He traced the shape against the sky, and she followed intently. Suddenly everything in her world seemed to hinge on finding those darn stars.

"Does it have a handle like this?" She traced a band of stars that might fit. Maybe. If she squinted, closed her left eye, and wished really hard.

His chest shook against her arm with laughter. She glowered at him. "Are you laughing at me?"

"I'm sorry. You should see your face."

She blew out a frosty breath. "Is it even up there, or were you just messing with me?"

"Yes, it's there. But it doesn't have a loopy handle."

"I told you I'm horrible at this," she complained, shoving

his shoulder.

The hum of the bus came from a distance. She met his eyes. "Well, it was nice knowing you."

"No. Please. Let me come see you tomorrow. I'll pick you up from work."

She wavered. Something stupid and foolish inside of her wanted to give him a chance, but the other louder—and smarter—part screamed to shove him away before it was too late. "I don't think that would be a good idea."

He clutched her hands, pulling them to his chest. "My father's will states I must marry within a given time, or I will lose all of my money."

She clenched his fingers tightly. So this was why he'd been so charming—so seemingly perfect? He wasn't a sweet man at all. No, he was schemer—just like all the other men in the world. "I fail to see how that affects me."

"I need to marry someone. But if I have to do such a thing, I want it to be on my terms. You care about the school. You're a good person. Together, we can take my money and put it to good use. Help out the poor people of the city, like you did tonight."

"I'm not marrying you. And I'm not for sale." Jerking her fingers free, she crossed her arms across her chest. Her body trembled with fury.

"I know you're not for sale. I am," he snapped, running a hand through his hair. "I'm just trying to be honest."

She ground her teeth together. "Right. And I honestly won't marry you."

"I'm asking you to listen to my proposal, and think about what I ask of you before answering. Please?"

"I've known you for a day. Why would I possibly marry

you?" She held up a hand. "And if you say for the money, I will kick you in the nuts."

Blanching, he drew in a deep breath. "Tomorrow, after work, I'll pick you up. We can discuss this once we've both have time to clear our heads."

"What's the point? My answer is no."

"Please. I know you don't know me well, but I promise I'm not crazy. Just give me a chance."

His eyes met hers, pleading. She hesitated.

"Fine." She threw her hands up. The bus pulled to a stop at the curb, hissing as its doors opened. She found her bus pass and flashed it at the driver. "Now, will you let me go home?"

"Yes," Damon said, eyes glowing with satisfaction. "What time do you finish work?"

"Four," she answered, rolling her eyes. "You're ridiculous, you know that, right?"

"Maybe. But I'll change your mind about me. Just wait and see."

"Mmhm."

He leaned in and brushed his lips across her cheek, and she fought the urge to sway closer. She shivered and caught her breath as he drew back. He captured her hand, squeezing it gently. "Until tomorrow."

She nodded and hurried away, climbing into the bus.

She had a terrible feeling that she'd somehow agreed to marry him without even knowing it.

Or wanting to.

• • •

Damon rolled over in bed, groaning at the incessant pounding in his skull. He'd never been a heavy drinker in the first place, and he'd buried his anger in booze last night after Johanna had refused him. Hell, who could blame him? He'd just found out he needed to get married to someone—anyone—in the next three months. Worse still, he needed to *stay* bloody married, and the one woman who made the idea seem appealing refused him.

Even from the grave, his father thwarted him. He'd covered every single angle he could have taken to avoid his father's last wishes. Now, Damon was left with a burning sensation in his gut and a sour taste in his mouth. As if the marriage stipulation weren't enough, he'd dared to throw in the other threat. The inconceivable one.

How dare his father force him into such a situation? How dare he make him be doomed to a life with a spoiled rich wife who couldn't care less whether he lived or died?

As swift as the anger came, guilt swept in and took control. Could he really be ranting at his deceased father? The man he missed more and more every day? It didn't seem... right.

But neither did marrying a woman for money.

He'd always thought that he would marry for love or not at all. Case closed.

Until now.

His father had managed to rip the case open and throw away the lid. Damn it. He scanned his memory for any other lady who'd thrown herself at him lately. Unfortunately, all he could picture was Johanna.

He had to win her over—the one woman who didn't want him.

Was that why she fascinated him so?

Maybe… Maybe he could lay his arguments out for her to see. Would marrying him be so hard for her?

Of course not. He'd just have to make the proposition irresistible.

Eyeing the clock, he hopped out of bed and headed directly for the Ibuprofen. He'd make charts. Graphs. Whatever type of visual crack she needed to get her to agree to marry him. Because some way, somehow, she would agree.

He wouldn't take no for an answer.

Chapter Four

Johanna juggled three totes full of crafts supplies, a purse, and a briefcase full of homework as she left the school. All of the other teachers, including Sara, had left half an hour ago. Johanna had needed more time to put away crayons and clean all the torn papers off the floor. Not to mention the glue the kids spilled all over their desks on a daily basis.

"Johanna," Damon called.

Johanna whirled. When she saw Damon, a tote slipped from her aching fingers. "Shit."

Arching a brow, he bent and retrieved the fallen bag, then plucked the other two from her grasp. The brisk breeze tousled his blond hair into disarray. "Is the 'shit' because of me or the bag?"

She flushed. "The bag, of course."

"Good to know. Here, I'll show you to my car."

She hesitated before following him. "I have work. Where are we going?"

"To my place, if that's okay." He clasped her shoulder, guiding her to a shiny black car.

"I really thought you would have changed your mind about—" She skidded to a halt. "Oh, God. Is that a Rolls-Royce? A Phantom?"

He gave her an odd look. "Yes. Why?"

"Why?" She took a deep breath, closing her eyes. She could buy a house for the amount of money he spent on a car. "No reason."

Damon strolled to the trunk and threw her belongings inside. A driver—an actual driver!—in a chauffeur's hat opened the door for her, smiling politely. She scooted inside, feeling awkward and clumsy.

"Oh my God. The leather feels butter-soft. Insane." She languished against the seat, running her fingers across the upholstery. When she glanced at Damon, she found him watching her with a heated stare. She couldn't believe she didn't burst into flames right then and there. "What?"

He shook his head, his jaw twitching as he averted his gaze and cleared his throat. "Nothing. I just like watching you."

"Oh." Warmth washed over her. No. *No.* She needed to knock it off. Stay cool. "You must not see a lot of women excited about leather, huh?"

"I guess not," he answered, mouth quirking. "How was your day? Kids all healthy?"

"In kindergarten? Yeah, right."

"How do you manage to avoid getting sick all of the time?"

She tapped her fingers on her knees. "I built up a resistance."

"What kind of lease do you have on your place?"

She blinked. "What? Why?"

"Curiosity. Is the lease a year to year thing?"

"Yes. My lease is up in a month." She pursed her lips. "But I'm not moving."

"I know," he mumbled.

When the driver opened the door, Damon climbed out after Johanna. She held her purse strap tightly, looking up at the mansion before her. The structure towered into the sky, the front faced in deep gray granite. She'd always loved stone houses, but never dreamed she'd ever actually be able to afford one. Most houses that looked like this were—and always would be—out of her reach.

Columns reached from the top of the house to the bottom, and a chimney puffed smoke, filling the air with the welcoming aroma of woodsmoke. She closed her eyes, savoring the scent. After the stodgy-looking butler opened the door for them and took their coats, Damon grabbed her hand and led her into an office with dark wood-paneled walls.

A chart was propped up in the corner, and she stepped closer, examining the paper. "Why does this have my name on it?"

Damon cleared his throat, leading her to a seat at a giant wooden table. "I'll get to that."

Her eyes widened, and she lurched to her feet as the pieces slipped into place. "Don't tell me you—"

He held out a hand. "You promised you would let me try to change your mind."

"And I also told you it would be useless. I can't believe you spent all this time making charts to convince me."

"You have a lot to gain from our agreement. It would

benefit you to hear me out."

"Fine. Speak." She crossed her legs, tapping her fingers on her knee. The picture behind him was crooked, and she fought the urge to fix it. He'd think she was crazy. Tearing her eyes from the imperfection, she focused on him.

He sighed. "So, I got a visit from my father's solicitor. The solicitor tells me there's another addendum to my father's will. One that was just discovered buried beneath some sub-clause."

She nodded. "What did he say?"

"He said if I don't get married in three months, I'll lose all of my money. All I'd have left of my father, if I fail to meet these demands, would be his title." Damon blew out a loud breath. "He always pressured me to settle down, take a wife. I would tease him and tell him I'd do it later, when I had the title and needed an heir. Apparently, he didn't trust me enough to follow through."

She clenched her fists. "Which is where you seem to think I come in. Don't you have some nice lady back home you're sweet on?"

Damon scoffed. "Nice lady? Those two words don't belong in the same sentence together. Not in my world."

"Is it even legal for someone to require you to marry these days?" She stood and paced, her mind racing. "It just seems so…antiquated."

"It is. I assume it's legal, since the lawyer didn't mention any possibility of fighting the addendum in court. I'm sure he would have informed me if the situation were otherwise."

"Speaking of which…why didn't you see this sub-clause?" she asked, leaning forward. "How did both you and a team of lawyers miss this?"

His gaze slid away from hers. "I've never really read the will."

Her eyes widened. "You've never read the will? Are you kidding me?"

"I have people who do that for me. Until now, they've done an excellent job," he said. He looked back at her tentatively. "I suppose this is God's way of showing me I need to get more involved in my personal affairs."

"You think?" She shook her head. "And your business, too. For someone with a lot of money, you sure are naïve about the way things work."

"I said I'd pay more attention. What more do you want from me?" He rubbed his eyes and released a drawn-out sigh. "I assure you, I've learned my lesson. Can we get back into the topic at hand—you marrying me?"

"Yeah, I guess." She shook her head. "So, when faced with this situation, you thought I'd be the best option? What gave you the impression that I was a money-grubbing whore?"

He blinked. "I don't think you are. That's why I want you."

"Well, you can't have me." She rose to her feet, rubbing her damp palms on her skirt. "There. Now you've narrowed down your list by one. Should make it a little easier, right?"

He shook his head, eyeing her. "If you say yes, then it would be easy."

"No. Go find some lady who worships you, explain the circumstances, then divorce. I'm sure she'd say yes if she was walking away holding some cash."

Arching a brow, he chuckled. "Are you insinuating I should buy myself a bride?"

"Sure. Why not? Gentlemen have been doing the same for years. Your ancestors included, I'd bet." She fought down distaste at the thought of him married to someone else. She had no right to those feelings—nor did she want them.

He ran a hand over his jaw. "The will states we must live together in matrimony for at least one year before any separation is allowed."

"Damn. He must have known you'd think of the fake marriage."

"He thought ahead on everything. Especially when it involved me."

"At least he didn't demand a baby, too."

"Oh, there's something about heirs in there. If the wife provides an heir, she will get a stipend for life. Extra incentive for her to drag me into bed with her greedy little claws, I suppose." He fisted his hands. "How could he do this to me?"

She couldn't help but admire the father's cunning, even if his methods were a little questionable. His outdated plan was beyond underhanded, but she had to give the man credit for thinking everything through.

"I'm sorry. Looks like you're gonna have to find a wife. And stop looking at me!" she snapped.

"Why?"

"People don't get married like this. There's supposed to be love. Commitment."

"You told me I should find a woman and ask her to marry me. Why is it okay for me to marry someone I don't love, but not acceptable for you?" He caught her wrist, drew her close, and caressed her cheek. "I know the ideal reason for marriage is love…but sometimes circumstances can change our dreams. Sometimes, we must make allowances."

"I guess," she answered uneasily. His gentle touch distracted her, making it hard to concentrate. Her stomach clenched when he licked his lips. Her eyes followed the dart of his tongue, focusing on the wet sheen it left behind.

"My parents married each other because their parents wanted them to. They were happy their whole lives. Did your parents love each other?" he asked.

"Huh?" Shaking her head, she forced her attention back to his words, instead of his mouth. "Maybe at some point. But not at the end."

"See?" he said, dropping his hand from her cheek. "Even when people marry for love, it falls apart more often than not. We would have a step up on the couples who marry for love. We will have rules. Expectations."

Oh, God. She almost wanted to say yes. Almost wanted to ease the torment haunting his eyes. This? Was bad. Really bad. With a grimace, she gestured to the easel. "When do the graphs and charts come into play in this whole mess?"

He tore his gaze from hers and sighed. "Okay. Exhibit A." He turned to the chart.

"I can't believe you actually did this."

He turned beet red, running his free hand through his hair. Clearing his throat, he charged onward. "There are three hundred and sixty-five days in a year. We would need to spend that long married, living together, to meet the terms of the will. If we manage to make it through the year without killing each other or going insane, you'd get an amount equal to a year's accumulation of my total net worth. My monthly income is here, in this section."

Her mouth dropped open. "You realize that's…" She

did some quick calculations. "…three million dollars, right?"

He nodded curtly. "In addition to said income, I'd also donate a million to a charity of your choice—such as the school—no questions asked. I'd also purchase a house of your choice, in your name only." He paused, flipping the page over. "We'd have to live here for now, in this house, due to my work. But since you'd be giving up your apartment, you wouldn't need to worry about the end of the year. This house is actually closer to the school. Shorter commute. No more buses."

"You really thought this through, didn't you?" she said, shaking her head. Graphs. He'd actually made graphs. She didn't know whether to laugh or kiss him. "Wow. Just… wow."

"It's the perfect solution. We've already established we, um, get along. I like you. The year will pass by quickly if you're by my side. And I know we could put my fortune to good use. You would make sure of it." He smiled, putting down the pointer he'd been using to sit beside her. "You'd have to attend social functions with me, naturally. All your clothing and jewelry will be completely covered. You need only show up."

"This is ridiculous. You're trying to pay me to marry you. Have you no pride?" She asked, exasperated. But she couldn't stop thinking what the million could do for the children in her school. Books. Computers. Supplies. Damn it, why did he have to put that in there? "Why charity? Why now? You could have donated at any time."

He ran a hand through his hair. "I checked you out on the Internet and saw how little funding these children get."

She held up a palm. "Hold up. You Googled me?

Really?"

"Actually…I used Bing."

She dropped her hand to her lap. "Oh for the love of—"

"But I saw how much they need help. All this time, I've been blind to the needs of others. I've had my head in the sand for too long. I want to help people—starting with the kids in your school."

Did he really, or was he just trying to win her over?

"So…you actually care? Or you're just bribing me?" She raised a brow. "Which is it?"

"Honestly?" He let out a loud sigh. "Both. I want you to say yes, and I want the children to have more books, and more supplies for the teachers."

"If I say no, will you still donate the money? Or is it dependent on my agreement?"

"If you say no, and I don't find anyone else to marry me, I won't have any money to donate. It'll go to some distant cousin in France that I've never even met."

"You could have anyone else you wanted for a lot less, I'm sure."

"I don't want anyone else. I want you." He clasped her hand. "If I have to do this, I want to do it on my terms. In my way."

"I think it's a horrible idea. Not to mention a waste of money. You could probably get someone to marry you for free."

"I'd pay even more to get you to say yes."

She shook her head. "You're insane. I'm going home now. My answer is—"

"Shh," he said, pressing a fingertip to her mouth. "Think about my proposition. Sleep on it. Don't answer me yet."

"It won't change anything."

"Maybe not. But I need you to say yes. It's the only way I'll make it through this mess intact." He took a deep breath. "We'll both know what to expect from the beginning. No secrets. No surprises."

When put that way, he sounded so...so right. Damn it. And the kids...

"I'll think about it." She hesitated, blushing. "This would be a marriage in name only, right?"

"I'd like to have a real marriage, in the bedroom. If you did. If not, we can work around your objections. Maybe." He grinned lopsidedly. "But I'd rather not."

She sighed, extricating herself from his arms. "I'm going home."

"I'll take you."

They headed outside into the cold. She couldn't help stealing a glance back at his house as he led her out the door. She loved the architecture, the stones, and the windows. Everything, really. Snow drifted from the sky. Damon cradled her hand in his, leading her to the car.

Her head spun, and she couldn't help but dwell on his proposition as she climbed into the car. It felt like a fairy tale. Too good to be true. But the things she could do with the money...

She could open a recreation center for underprivileged kids. Help get the school out of debt and into budget. The possibilities were endless.

When they were almost to her apartment, she looked away from the window to find Damon staring at her, smiling widely.

"You're thinking about us, aren't you?" he asked,

scooting closer. "I can see the wheels turning."

She hesitated, not meeting his eyes. "Are the terms negotiable?"

"Of course," he answered immediately. "What do you want? More money?"

"Yes. No." She bit her lip, looking out the window. "I want to reverse the numbers. Three million to charity. One to me."

He sucked in a deep breath, his hands tightening on his knees. "Let me get this straight. You want less money? That's your bargaining chip?"

"Mmhm."

"I don't think there is anyone in this world who has a cleaner conscience than you. You're incredible."

She flushed, waving a hand in the air. "No, I'm not. Anyone else would—"

"Anyone else would ask for more. For them, not others."

"Whatever. I'll marry you." She felt a weight lift off her shoulders. She'd be helping kids with the money he'd donate for charity. He'd have a wife so he could keep his money.

"Thank you!" He captured her hand and pulled it to his chest. "I'm going to make you a very, very happy girl for the next year. I promise I'll make you feel like a bloody princess."

"I already do."

A hollow feeling crept into her gut. She needed to remember this was temporary. Short term. She must, at all times, guard her heart. With a Glock, if need be.

The car pulled to a stop in front of her building, and he swept her into his arms, his lips closing in on hers with alarming speed.

"No kissing," she reprimanded, pulling out of his embrace. "This is business, not pleasure."

He nodded, his eyes dropping. "I'll do all the planning. Do you want a real wedding, or a small justice ceremony?"

"Small. The wedding's not real, after all."

He set her down and ran a hand through his hair. His voice was brittle. "Right. Of course."

"When will we get married?"

"I'll draw up the contracts tomorrow. Make sure all the bases are covered, and then we'll do it. Sound good?"

"Mmhm."

"Good. Until tomorrow…" He shook her hand, his eyes searching hers. "Please tell me this won't be a marriage in name only."

"Fine. I won't tell you." Shrugging, she headed inside. She stole one last glance at him before she shut the door. "Good night, Damon."

"Good night, Johanna."

Chapter Five

Damon stood beside the justice of the peace, his palms sweating and his mind racing. In minutes, she'd become his bride. He couldn't believe he'd gotten her to agree. He had a sneaking suspicion that if he hadn't added in the charity donation, she'd have laughed her way out of his office—and out of his life.

Yesterday, while signing the contract, she obsessed over the charity details, but barely glanced at the section naming her gains. On anyone else, he'd think her actions were a front to hide her true greed. On Johanna, however, he knew it wasn't an act.

If he wasn't careful, at the end of the year she'd leave with more than money and a house—she'd leave with his heart.

Good thing he had no intention of giving it to her.

Johanna stepped into the room and desire punched straight through his chest. She wore a deep burgundy cotton

dress with shimmery black edging. The dress flowed grace-
fully to her knees. The neckline skimmed across her cleavage, and he yearned to caress her soft skin. Her hair swept
her shoulders, left down for the occasion instead of her usual
ponytail. He took a step closer to her, palms itching with the
need to touch her. To make her his.

"You look—you look—"

"Gorgeous," her friend Sara finished. She grinned,
punching him in the shoulder. "Couldn't help but notice you
seemed at a loss for words."

Jeff chuckled. "Enjoy the silence while it lasts."

Damon met Johanna's eyes, reveling in her blush. She
looked down at her clasped hands. He strode to her side,
grasping her hand. "Shall we get married?"

Johanna let out a little nervous laugh. "Yeah. Why the
hell not?"

"Indeed. Why the hell not?"

He couldn't think of a single reason.

• • •

Don't say yes, Johanna prayed. *Wait…say it. I don't know.*
She almost wished the justice of the peace would sense it
was all a sham and call it off.

"I do," Damon said, without a moment's hesitation.
Johanna clenched her fists to keep from wiping her sweaty
palms on her dress.

Now it was her turn.

All the times she'd pictured her wedding day, it had been
nothing like this. No one stood by her side except Sara. No
mother or father cried in each other's arms as their baby

got married. Sara was the only person she'd told about the wedding. No one in her family even knew—or cared.

The justice of the peace cleared his throat. Johanna flinched. He quirked his brows, and her face heated. "I'm sorry. What did you say?"

He cleared his throat. "I said, do you take this man as your lawfully wedded husband?"

"Uh." She met Damon's eyes. "I…"

Damon squeezed her hand. "We'll be all right."

She swallowed heavily. "I do."

As soon as she said the words, the rest of the world seemed to fade away, and she couldn't take her eyes off of Damon. His glowing gaze swept over her and her chest tightened. Her body trembled. Before she knew it, the justice of the peace said, "You may now kiss the bride."

Damon grinned, pulling her into his arms. He pressed his mouth to her ear and asked, "Am I allowed to kiss you now?"

She shivered. His hot breath did things to her constitution she'd rather not explore. She pressed her lips together tightly. "Quick. No tongue."

He chuckled. "Yes, ma'am."

He kissed her softly, chastely, pulling away almost immediately. His hands lingered on her waist before they, too, dropped away. His eyes burned with desire as he locked gazes with her. Her stomach wrenched with an intensity that downright scared her.

Stay professional. Stay focused. She had to remember this was business, even if he forgot.

Perhaps this marriage wouldn't be so easy and clear-cut after all.

• • •

Johanna perched on the edge of her new bed, fingering the hem of her skimpy nightgown. Though they hadn't spoken about what would happen tonight, she knew Damon would be coming to the room soon. Shrugging into a heavy robe, she tied the belt securely. There hadn't been much chance to talk throughout the day, but the time had come to lay it all on the line.

There would be no sex.

She'd promised to love, honor and cherish him—but only for a year. She knew their time had an expiration date. She couldn't let him in too far.

The door creaked open and Damon hovered in the doorway. The top three buttons of his shirt were undone, and his tie was missing. His feet were bare, and he held two glasses and a bottle of champagne.

"May I come in?"

"Yes. Of course." She stood and met him halfway. She tried to smile, but ended up grimacing, her mouth twisting nervously. Smooth. Real smooth. When she removed the glasses from his hands, their fingers brushed. She quivered at the contact. "Champagne?"

"Hm?" He shook his head a little, focusing on her once more. "Oh. Yes."

While he busied himself pouring, she studied him. He had made so many of her dreams come true. So many things she never thought she'd be able to give to the community now stood in front of her. She couldn't believe her luck. How had she managed to come across such a good guy?

And why had he chosen her?

Fool.

"I have to tell you something before you get the wrong idea," she blurted, tugging on the robe to her belt.

Sighing, he handed her a glass. "You don't want to have sex."

She blinked. "Uh, right. How did you know?"

He cast a look over her body, twisting his lips in a mockery of a smile. "That foul robe."

She tugged the belt tighter. "I don't want to hurt you, but this has to stay professional and proper. Or else someone will get hurt. I'm sorry."

His smile turned strained. "It's okay. I'm fine with us, uh, keeping our distance."

"Oh. Good."

"But…" He captured her hand, pulling her close to his chest. He cupped her cheek. "I'm going to do everything in my power to make you change your mind."

She savored the feel of his hand on her cheek. She wished she could do it. Longed to say yes. She swayed closer. His breath fanned across her cheeks, stroking her skin to sensitivity—and reality, cold bitch that she was, slapped her across the face. She needed to back off—now.

She shook her head and shrugged loose. Would it be so wrong to succumb and enjoy him for a year? Would she be able to keep her heart detached?

Not possible. With him all the normal rules seemed to leave the building. Hell, she'd married him. If that didn't define pure craziness, she had no clue what did.

"I won't change my mind. I'm quite good at avoiding seduction, I'll have you know."

He raised his eyebrows, and his lips slanted into a smile. "Oh? So, if I kissed you, you would be fine?"

"More than fine." She tried to keep her face calm, though her body ached at the mere thought of his lips on hers. Her mouth suddenly felt dry, her tongue in need of champagne. She sipped at it, eyeing him. "Not that I'm saying you should."

"Oh, but I will," he said, eyes glowing with determination. He took the champagne flute out of her hand, set it down, and wrapped her in his arms. Her heart skipped a beat and her hands clutched his shirt.

He plundered her mouth, his tongue stroking hers. His hands gripped her hips, pulling her close. She whimpered low in her throat, eagerly returning his kiss. With a groan, he tore his mouth away, breathing heavily. He rested his forehead against hers. Their breaths melded into one as she fought to regain control of her mind.

"Not a problem, right?" he breathed, his hold tightening on her hips before he released her. He shoved his hands into his pockets. She couldn't take her eyes off his moist lips. She ached to taste them again. "Uh, Johanna?"

She snapped to attention, her cheeks heating. "Perhaps we shouldn't try that again."

He grinned. "Too much?"

"No. I just don't want to kiss you anymore. It's a bad idea for business partners."

"We could be more," he said, gaze dropping to her lips.

"I'm not going to change my mind. Business. Not pleasure."

"Hm." He saluted her with his glass. "Challenge accepted."

Chapter Six

Damon knocked on Johanna's bedroom door. His nerves threatened to bring him to his knees. He'd meant it when he said he would woo her—and win. Tonight marked phase one: date night.

He held his breath until she opened the door. Her cheeks were rosy and her eyes bright. What had she been doing? Over her shoulder, he could see that the TV on the wall was paused.

"What are you watching?" he asked.

She threw a guilty glance at the screen and then met his eyes. "A Lifetime movie."

He choked on a laugh. "Christ. It's true, isn't it? All women are addicted to those things."

Throwing the door the rest of the way open, she chuckled. She headed for the bed, flopped onto her stomach, and cradled her chin in her hands. "Hey, at least if you try to hire a thug to kill me, I'll see all of the warning signs. Unlike this fool."

He walked to the side of the bed. If only he could lie down next to her, he'd be a happy man. Hell, he would even willingly watch crappy movies if it meant being with her. "I assure you that I will do no such thing."

"That's what he said." She gestured at the TV and hit play. "She believed him."

He watched for a minute before he rolled his eyes. "I'm starting to see why he'd be tempted. She's annoying."

"So he should kill her?" she scoffed.

"Well, perhaps not kill her." He grinned. "Maybe divorce her, though."

"Since I know you didn't come in here to watch a movie with me...what's up?" She clicked pause and rolled onto her side.

"We're going out tonight."

She blinked. "Is it one of those social things you mentioned before or something? I don't remember you telling me about it."

"No." He cleared his throat and shifted. "It's a date."

Her eyes narrowed. "A date? Why?"

"I'm determined to make you like me," he said.

"Why?"

"Because I like you." He straightened his shirt sleeves and fidgeted with the cuffs. "It's just a date."

She ran her fingers through her hair. "I don't know about this. It seems like a bad idea."

"It seems like a bad idea to have fun on a Saturday night? That seems awfully convoluted. It's just an outing. I promise I won't throw myself at you—without explicit permission, anyway."

"Well…when you put it that way…"

He grinned. "See you at eight."

. . .

Johanna smoothed her ponytail and sighed. She'd been an idiot to agree to this. A complete fool. Deranged. She had a date with her fake husband. How much more messed up could they possibly get? But even so, excitement made her shaky.

Where would he take her? Would he try to kiss her? If he thought she'd be easy, he was wrong. She might be up for a fun friendship, but that's all. The sooner he realized as much, the better off they would both be.

"Johanna, are you ready?" he called through the door.

She smoothed her hair one last time before snatching her purse and hurrying to the door. When she swung it open, he grinned at her and held up a red rose. "For you, my lady."

Damn it. "Thank you. It's lovely."

She took the rose, making sure not to touch his fingers. If she let herself touch him, all common sense would fly out the window. She brought the rose to her nose. The sweet fragrance washed over her, and she looked into his eyes.

"I was torn between a rose and a tulip. A rose is more romantic…but you seem to not want romance from me," he said.

His intense stare sent a jolt of molten heat through her. Screw coffee. She was awake. Definitely awake.

"You thought correctly," she murmured. She tore her gaze from his and gulped a deep breath of air. Why was she so damn lightheaded? "I'm not interested in romance."

"Yet you seem to like that rose quite a bit." When she said nothing, he chuckled. "Are you ready?" He offered his arm and she slipped her palm into the crook. Their upper arms brushed against each other as they walked.

"Where are we going?" she asked.

"You'll see."

She looked at him out of the corner of her eye. "Really? We're gonna play that game?"

He gave a one shouldered shrug. "Game? I've no idea what you mean. But I'm not telling you where we're going, if you're asking me that."

The night air slapped her in the face as they left the house, and she gave in to temptation and swayed closer to Damon's warmth while they waited for the car to come to the door. He grinned at her when she melded against his body.

"Don't look at me like that." She squinted up at the sky. "I'm cold, not in love."

"Ouch." He patted her hand. "Let's not forget blunt and honest."

"Oh, look. The car's here."

"Nice change of subject."

"Thank you."

The car pulled to a stop and they climbed in. After about ten minutes of tense silence, and a lot of anxious fidgeting on her part, the car took the ramp off the highway.

"Hm. Interesting," she mumbled. Ducking her head, she scanned the signs on the exit ramp.

"Figure it out yet?" he asked. She looked at him, only to find he'd moved closer to her. His eyes were mere inches from hers. Had they always been so gorgeous?

She swallowed a large gulp of air. "Well, there's a mall, a hospital, and a museum. I'm guessing we're going to the museum."

"You'd be correct," he answered. He ran a finger over her jaw line and then touched her nose. "You've got beauty and brains. The whole package."

She rolled her eyes. "Yep. That's me."

The car stopped at the Museum of Science. When the driver opened the door, they climbed out, and Damon pulled her close to his side. She shot him a dirty look, and he blinked innocently. "What? I'm cold, not in love."

Her lips quirked against her will. "You're ridic—"

He touched a finger to her lips. "—ulous," he finished, his voice husky. "Yes, I know. You've told me."

She swayed closer. Her chest brushed against his, snapping her out of her trance, and she pulled away.

"So what are we doing here? Art? Science?"

"Constellations," he said.

"What?" She groaned. "You just want to make fun of me again, don't you?"

"I wouldn't do that." He paused. "All right, maybe I would. But this is different. It's a program that shows you the constellations in the sky, and shows you how to find them. It even customizes it to what is in the sky tonight— not just any time of year. After this, you'll be able to walk out and see them."

She blinked. "Wow. Okay. You seem awfully excited about this."

His ears turned pink. Good God, even when the man blushed he was adorable.

They got in line and he shuffled his feet. "Yeah. I

thought you'd like it. If you'd rather do something else, we can. Movie? Dinner?"

"No," she said. "It's perfect. I love it."

His eyes lit up. "Good. Come on. Let's go learn about the stars."

• • •

Damon practically dragged Johanna out the doors. She'd been silent through the whole presentation, concentrating harder than everyone else in the room combined. Her attention had never wavered from the fake sky. Each time she'd found a constellation, a smile had tugged at her lips—and tugged at his heart.

Hell, he'd barely heard a word the presenter had said. His gaze had been firmly on her.

Her head tilted up to the sky as they left the building. "Oh," she said, a wondering smile lighting her face. "I see it. I see Puppis."

He followed her eyes and nodded. "Yes, that's it."

Her head brushed his arm. "And Cancer. I see that, too."

"Mmhm." His gaze locked on her face. "It's gorgeous."

"It is," she breathed. Her gaze slid to his and she froze.

He tried to say something witty or light. But seeing her here, outside under the stars, took all conscious thought away. If he tried to speak, he'd sound like a blubbering idiot.

Instead he cupped her cheek, tugged her close, and pressed his lips to hers.

He kept his touch light. She resisted him at first, pulling back, but then she fisted her hands in his jacket and drew him closer. Tonight was not about seduction or sex. No, he had a larger goal in mind—and hopping into bed was not it.

Somehow, he tore his lips from hers. She moaned low in her throat, and he almost succumbed to the temptation to kiss her again. He ran his thumb over her damp lower lip, aching to taste her one more time.

"Hungry?" he breathed softly.

"Huh?" She blinked up at him. Her breaths escaped into the cold air like smoke.

He smiled down at her. "I said, are you hungry?"

"Mm." Looking up at the sky, she sighed. "We shouldn't be doing this. It's a mistake."

"No, a mistake would be not doing this. I want this. I want you."

"You don't. Not really," she whispered. "You don't even know me. You just think you do."

He tugged at her hand. She met his eyes reluctantly. "Then tell me about you. Tell me what I need to know."

"There's no point. This is business, not pleasure." She yanked her hand free and strode to the car.

He shook his head and followed her in grim silence. When he slid into the car, he started to speak, but his phone cut him off. When he heard the ringtone, his mouth went dry.

He pulled the cell out of his pocket, brought it to his ear, and said, "Hello?"

At the sound of the voice on the other end, he forgot all about Johanna.

"Damon?"

· · ·

Johanna watched Damon's car disappear down the driveway.

Once she couldn't see it any longer, she sighed and headed to the kitchen for more coffee. He'd gone for a "meeting" with the person who'd called him last night.

The person who had made him smile, and caused his eyes to light up. At least, he'd been excited until he saw Johanna watching him. Then he'd completely shut down. Which probably meant the caller was a woman.

When she wandered out into the foyer, the butler entered from the opposite direction.

He paused and bowed. "My lady."

"Johanna," she corrected for what had to be the hundredth time. "Sorry to bother you, but does Damon go on these meetings often?"

"Yes, my lady. Every Sunday."

"Oh." She tightened her grip on her coffee mug. "Do you know how long he's usually gone?"

The butler gave a terse nod. "Usually about two or three hours, my lady."

"Oh." She hesitated. Was she so desperate for information that she'd bug the butler? "Tell me, do you know where he goes?"

He backed up and pinched his lips tightly. "I'm not certain, my lady. If you'll excuse me, I hear a maid calling me."

The butler fled. Please, the man knew when Damon missed a shave, for the love of God. Surely he knew where he went every single Sunday.

The butler was obviously in on the secret. Whoever Damon went to see on Sundays—and she could only guess it was a woman—was important enough to rank a private ringtone, and secrecy.

Interesting. Very interesting.

Chapter Seven

Damon sat as his desk, poring over account numbers. Johanna stole a glance at him before returning her attention to grading papers. The past two months had passed in a blur. In the mornings, her driver dropped her off at school, and when she finished her day at work, the driver would take her home. Then, in the evening, she'd settle in his office to work on grading papers and setting up her lesson plans while he worked on his own business affairs.

She yawned and looked at her watch. "It's almost eight o'clock. Want to break for some dinner?"

Damon blinked, focusing on her. "Give me five more minutes. I'm almost finished with this column."

She smiled, shaking her head as he turned his attention back to the papers on his desk. "For someone who hated doing anything business related, you sure seem to be hooked on 'one more minute' now. You sound like an addict."

He chuckled, but didn't glance up. "Hey, just doing my

job."

She sighed and placed a star and a sticker on the paper in front of her. Her stomach rumbled, but she didn't say another word. His new interest in his company thrilled her. Like hell she'd interrupt for something like food.

"Ah ha," he called out. "There it is."

She looked up. "There what is?"

"The shipments from last month were all off. I couldn't figure out why we were missing not only goods, but money. Someone entered the delivery as a shipment instead of received goods." He smiled at her. "Everything adds up perfectly now."

"Good," she said, returning his smile. "I'm glad you figured it out."

"I never thought I'd enjoy maths so much, but damn that feels good." He intertwined his fingers behind his head and leaned back in his desk chair. "I've discovered I'm actually pretty good at maths. Who knew?"

"It doesn't surprise me," she murmured, setting down the stickers. "You've got a good head on you. You just weren't using it."

"Gee, thanks. You're too kind."

Grinning, she stood. "Does that mean we get to eat now? I'm starving."

He chuckled and rose as well. "I noticed. I thought someone let a small dog in the house."

"Hey, now. I can't help it if I need food." She punched his shoulder. "It's your fault for having such an amazing cook."

"She loves to show off for you, too," he said. When they entered the dining room, he gestured at the table. "Check out the display tonight."

Red and pink candles lined the center of the table, bathing the room in their soft glow. At their entry, a servant left and Damon led her to her customary spot. He seated himself and smiled at her. She sipped her wine.

"You have glitter on your nose." He swiped it away. His touch, though innocent enough, made her stomach clench. "There. All gone."

"Thanks," she mumbled, dropping her gaze to her lap. Damn him for being so cute. "I wonder what we're having tonight."

He sank back into his chair. "I've heard a rumor it's roast."

"Mm." She rubbed her growling stomach. "Excellent."

"Says the alleged vegetarian…"

She chuckled. "I know. I'm mean."

His cell rang and he glanced at the caller ID. "Hello?"

She tensed. She knew that ringtone. She'd heard it at the planetarium. She'd heard it every Saturday since. It was assigned to one person and one person only—the woman he visited every Sunday. He laughed, and jealousy gnawed at her. She had no idea who the mystery woman was—but she could certainly venture a guess.

"I'll come see you on Sunday. Remember?" He caught sight of Johanna watching him and flushed. Pulling the phone away from his mouth, he said, "Excuse me. I'll be right back."

She nodded and forced a smile.

The servant carried their food in, bringing with him the scent of beef and potatoes, but she was no longer hungry. She could think only of Damon, and the woman who made him so happy.

He returned, sniffing. "Mm. That smells delicious. Sorry I had to excuse myself."

"No worries." She took a sip of wine and tilted her head. "Who was it?"

"Oh, just a friend. We have a meeting on Sunday." He turned red and picked up his fork. She watched him eat, but made no move to do the same.

She couldn't stand it any longer. "A meeting? Again?"

He put the fork down and crossed his arms. "Yes. Every Sunday. Remember when I told you I have a meeting scheduled every week?"

She swallowed heavily. "Yeah. Sorry. Must've slipped my mind."

Though he resumed eating, his eyes remained on her. "Aren't you going to eat?"

She picked up her fork and stabbed a potato. Though cooked to perfection, it tasted flat and dull. She pushed back from the table and rose. "I'm not hungry anymore. I think I'm going to go to bed."

He raised a brow and stood. "At eight-thirty on a Friday night?"

Her ears must be on fire, judging from the burning sensation. "Uh, yeah. Good night."

"Are you okay?" he asked.

"Fine," she snapped.

She fled the room and didn't stop until she was safely ensconced behind her bedroom door. He had a meeting every Sunday afternoon, did he? Oh, it was a meeting all right. But not the type he implied.

If she were his wife in every way, she would've nagged him until he confessed the truth behind his trips. But, as his business partner…she let it drop. As much as it killed her.

Though she told herself it was only natural for him to seek out his pleasure elsewhere, since she herself gave him none, she couldn't help but feel heartbroken. Which only served to anger her more. Hello, she'd told him she would not—could not—give him sex. What the hell did she expect the man to do…become a eunuch?

He was far too gorgeous to suffer such a fate.

• • •

The next morning, she woke with his mysterious Sunday meetings still on her mind. In fact, the bitch had haunted her dreams. She rolled out of bed, brushed her teeth, and descended the stairs.

When she walked into the dining room, she found Damon dressed and waiting for her. She halted and studied him.

"Hello." She sought out caffeine before she hurt someone—namely her obnoxiously energetic husband.

"Good morning," He grinned and held out a mug of coffee.

"Ah. Thank you." She inhaled the aroma, and already the world felt like it made more sense. "So, what are we doing today? I see you're ready to go."

He fidgeted and dropped his gaze to his feet. "Well…I thought we would volunteer today. If you don't mind," he added.

"Where?"

"The soup kitchen."

"I'd love that."

"Good. And then after, I have another surprise planned for you."

She groaned. "You really won't give up, will you?"

"Nope. I'm determined to win you over. You are my wife, after all."

"Business partner."

"Eat breakfast, and then we'll go. I have to finalize our arrangements for tonight." Rubbing his hands together, he left the room with a grin on his face. She laughed and sank into her seat at the table.

As she ate, she wondered what they would be doing after feeding the poor. He managed to surprise her more and more with each "date," and she suspected this time would be no exception. She really didn't understand him. Saturdays he lavished attention on her, stopping at nothing to make her happy. He acted as if the world revolved around her, and all he wanted out of life was her love. Her trust.

The two things she refused to give him.

And then, in a complete reversal, on Sunday he abandoned her for his booty call. Every. Single. Week.

Sighing, she exited the dining room. Damon was in the foyer, directing servants to carry out garment bags full of clothing.

She pursed her lips. "Do I get to know why we need a change of clothing?"

"Nope."

"You're ridiculous sometimes."

"Perhaps. Are you ready to go feed the hungry?"

She brushed her hair out of her eyes and pulled it into a tight ponytail. "Sure. And then we are…?"

"Going somewhere else. Come on." He grinned and

strode out the door without waiting for a response.

. . .

Damon served the last person in line and swiped sweat from his forehead. Unfortunately, all it really accomplished was to make him even stickier. He never felt as unattractive and foul as he did in this moment—but he'd never been so bloody satisfied, either. Every grateful smile thrown his way from the homeless, every sidelong glance shared with Johanna, combined until his heart threatened to burst.

Speaking of which...

Johanna set down the empty plate she carried and strolled toward him, smiling from ear to ear. He straightened, tearing the hideous hairnet off and wiping his hands on his apron.

"Hey, put it back on," she protested. "You looked hot."

He grinned and smoothed his hair. He ached to touch her. To kiss her. Hell, at this point he would settle for a bloody kiss on the cheek.

"Oh?" he teased, tugging it back on his head. "Well, in that case, come a little closer, or I'll smack you with my wooden spoon."

She swatted his hands away. "I think we can go now. Our job is over."

The door opened and he sighed. "Nope, here comes another one."

She smiled at the woman approaching—and froze. An odd expression came over her face and she paled. "Mom?"

"What?" He glanced at the woman, then back at Johanna. He could see no resemblance whatsoever. "That's your mother?"

The woman stumbled forward, hand outstretched. "Is that you, Johanna?"

Johanna gave a curt nod. "When did you come back?"

The woman rubbed her dirty nose, shuddering. Damon couldn't believe this shell of a woman could be his Johanna's mother. There was no mistaking the track marks up her arms.

Her mother darted a look at him before returning her greedy eyes to her daughter. "A few days ago. I got tired of Vegas. I went by your place, but they said you moved."

Johanna glanced at Damon, blushing. "Could you excuse us, please?"

Swallowing hard, he nodded. "Certainly."

He backed away, but could still make out snippets of conversation. Her mother asked for money, and Johanna headed to her purse. Returning to her mother's side, she handed her mother a check and patted her shoulder.

Of their own accord, his feet inched closer. He picked up a spoon and stirred the remaining gravy before sliding even closer to check on the corn.

"Remember, I'll send money to your apartment manager once you pick a place. Just make sure you call the number on the check and let me know where you are. Okay?" Johanna asked.

"Yeah. I'll let you know." Her mother scurried out of the room with the check clutched close to her chest. Johanna bit her lip.

Damon clenched his jaw and rubbed her shoulders. There was obviously more to Johanna's resistance than playing hard to get. Could he somehow break through the barriers her obviously drugged-up mother had helped erect?

Damn right he could. He didn't have a choice, not if he wanted to succeed in his plan to save everything in his life that mattered to him.

"Are you all right?"

Sighing, she shook her head and turned away. "Can we go now?"

He squeezed her shoulder. "All right. Let me talk to the owner before we leave."

She nodded and retreated, heading out the back door. He watched her walk away, his heart heavy.

• • •

Johanna watched Damon through the window as he wrote out a check and handed it off to the ecstatic owner of the shelter. He'd probably donated enough to keep the kitchen open for a year. He came out of the building and shoved his hands in the pockets of his coat.

"Ready?" he asked, his voice heavy.

She nodded and followed him to the car. Knowing he'd seen her mother—and what her mother was—made her queasy. Once seated, she stared out the window. Maybe he would finally realize that she was damaged goods, not worth the trouble.

"What happened with your mother?" he asked quietly.

The car rolled into motion. "Are you sure you want to know? It's not pretty."

"Of course I want to know. It's what makes you…you." He clasped her hand.

"…Fine." She exhaled heavily and looked out the window. If she had to say this, she couldn't look at him. "When

I turned twelve, my father left us. My mother was a drug addict, and he couldn't take the stress anymore. I don't blame him. If given a choice, I'd have left, too."

"He left you with a mother who couldn't provide for you?"

She hesitated, nodding.

"She had a job, but she spent all her money on drugs. When I was thirteen, a family friend gave me work, helping him at his convenience store. If not for him, I would have starved to death. He rented us an apartment over his store for cheap, taking the fee out of my paycheck."

"Christ," he murmured. His grip tightened on her hand. "That must have been so hard for a kid your age to handle."

She rubbed her forehead. "Well, yeah. It was. I hid all the money I earned, so my mom wouldn't steal it for drugs. She'd get so mad at me when I refused to give her the cash. She had a mean right hook."

Damon clenched his fists. "I didn't know."

"I'm not done yet," she blurted. She needed him to hear this. To understand why she couldn't let him in. "When I was sixteen, she ran away with all the money I'd saved. I had nothing for rent. Nothing for food. I ended up getting another job waitressing. Between the two jobs and high school, I didn't sleep much. I got scholarships, went to college. All my life, I've been on my own."

He shook his head and leaned back against the car seat. "You're amazing. You know that?"

"No," she breathed. She dropped her forehead into her palm. Tears blurred her vision. "I'm really not. I'm broken and I can't love anyone. I can't get close to another person— can't let them in. No one. Not friends, not family…not you."

"Why are you telling me this?"

She closed her eyes. "Because I won't give in." So he could stop the Saturday dates, stop the charming smiles, stop…everything. Just stop, now that he knew how broken she was. "I won't fall in love. Love is weak and fleeting. I can't rely on it."

"Then don't," he answered, capturing her hand. "But you can rely on me. We might not be in love, but I promise you that I'm here, whenever you need me."

"I don't know what to say," she whispered, avoiding his eyes.

"I do." After giving her hand one last squeeze, he let go. She missed his warmth the instant he released her. And worse yet, she missed his support. His excited tone rang false. "We're almost there. Ready for part two of our date?"

She tried to dredge up some of her previous excitement, and shoved the encounter with her mother from her mind. "Where are we going?"

"A hotel."

She crossed her arms over her chest. "Really? Do you think getting me in a room alone will help you win me over? I assure you, I have more control than that."

"We will share a room, but with separate sleeping quarters. There will be more to our stay than sleeping."

God, he'd actually admitted that he meant to seduce her. Even worse, her traitorous bitch of a body quivered at the thought. "Damon, I told you—"

"You misread my intentions," he said. "Patience, my dear. You will see our destination soon enough."

"Are we spending the night?" she asked, and fidgeted with her jacket.

"Yes. I booked the honeymoon suite." He smoothed his hair. "If that's okay with you, of course."

"Mmhm. What about your, uh…" She fretted her hands. "…'meeting' you always have on Sunday?"

He tensed, cheeks flushing as he tugged at his tie. "I'll still make it on time."

"Maybe you could skip it this week?"

His eyes darted away from hers and focused somewhere over her head. "No. I can't."

"Oh. Right." She bit her lip—and her tongue. She would not ask what he did every Sunday. She had pride. Self-esteem. Not to mention control of her emotions. "Where do you go?"

Son of a bitch.

"To visit a friend," he mumbled. Pointing out the window, he flashed a tight smile. "Oh, look! We're here!"

Her heart plummeted. What had she really expected him to say, though? Theirs wasn't a real marriage, but it would still break man-code if he admitted he had a mistress. Feigning excitement, she bent low to look out his window. A grandiose hotel loomed high into the sky, more elegant than any building she'd ever seen.

Awe was a light and airy thing inside her chest. "Wow," she breathed. "It's gorgeous."

"It is," he agreed. She glanced his way and found his attention not on the building, but on her. The longing and desire in his eyes knotted a fist of tension to her stomach, clenching her tightly in its grasp. Why did he look at her like that when he had a relationship with someone else? How could he?

His hot gaze left her mouth dry. They parked at the

entrance and she read the billboard on the sidewalk.

Her eyes widened as she skimmed over the announcements. Spinning to face him, she laughed. "No! You didn't!"

"Oh, I certainly did. We're going to a ball," he announced. "I do believe I owe you a waltz."

"Oh! And it's a costume ball. That's what is in the garment bags, isn't it? Costumes?" She jumped out of the car. This would be the best date ever.

He strode to her side, his arm brushing hers. "I see you're happy with my surprise."

"Happy?" She launched herself into his arms, hugging him tightly. He held her close to his chest. Drawing back, she looked up into his eyes.

There it was again. The desire. An answering need rose within her, refusing to be denied any longer. Burning inside her, reaching higher and higher. Her resistance was crumbling at an alarming rate. She gritted her teeth. No, damn it. She couldn't give in to temptation.

Clearing her throat, she extricated herself from his arms and whispered, "Thank you."

He gave her a smoldering look, his fingers flexing at his sides, but offered his arm and escorted her inside.

• • •

Damon tugged at his cravat, casting a covert glance in Johanna's direction. Her eyes were wide and her cheeks flushed, but she gripped his elbow tightly. She looked absolutely ravishing in her eighteenth-century ball gown. Her muslin dress was topped with a dusty rose print, which split down the front to reveal the under layer of pink. The dress's neckline left little to the imagination. He forced his gaze away, as a proper gentleman should.

At least tomorrow he would get to see Lilly. He couldn't bloody wait to lose himself in Lilly's laugh.

Johanna tugged the neckline up. "Do you know how to waltz? I don't. It's not exactly something they taught us in public school."

"I know what to do. Just follow my lead," he assured her, squeezing her hand. *And…if I lead you into the bedroom, just strip. Simple.* "It'll be fun."

"Okay."

The orchestra cued up, and as one the partygoers all headed onto the dance floor. Damon led Johanna to an open space, placing her before him. Excitement and nervousness darted across her face; he smiled. Her gaze flitted over the dancers surrounding them.

"Did you know that the waltz was once considered too bold for the ballroom? It was thought to be a form of seduction, too risqué for a debutante."

"Good thing I'm not a debutante, then," she whispered in his ear, her hot breath sending every last drop of blood straight south.

Her fingers shook in his, but her eyes twinkled. His breath caught in his throat. Gorgeous. Enticing. And his, if only briefly. "First I bow." He bowed at his waist, never taking his eyes from hers. "And then you curtsy."

With a smile, she dipped into a flawless curtsy. Her eyes enthralled him, and he swallowed heavily.

Anticipation made his palms sweaty as he held his hand out to her and said, "Excellent! Put your hand in mine." When she slid her hand into his, he pulled her into his arms.

"Now put your other hand here, on my arm, right under my shoulder."

He clasped her side, right next to her breast and under her arm. She jerked, cheeks flushing when his palm brushed bare flesh.

"A-are you sure that's right?" she asked, exhaling. She glanced around them. "Oh. It is."

Leaning down, he pressed his cheek to hers and whispered, "Now do you see why it was forbidden?"

She nodded. "Yes."

"Hm," he breathed, rubbing his cheek against hers before pulling back into position. "Now, I take two steps back, and we take off."

"What?"

Her eyes widened when he began to spin her in elaborate circles across the ballroom. No matter what happened in the next year, he would never forget this moment. Her laughter as they twirled down the dance floor washed over him. He whipped her around the room, taking every opportunity he could to pull her even closer to his body until her breasts brushed against his chest. If he had any luck left, he'd kept her too busy for her to notice everyone else danced at a more respectable distance.

He danced her into the shadows, concealing her from curious onlookers.

She glanced past his shoulder, eyebrows raised. "Um, why are we back here?"

"Because I promised you an authentic waltz. Do you know what usually happened when a rakish earl danced with a lady he desired?" He trailed a finger down over her jaw line. The softness of her skin taunted him. He ached to touch every last inch of her…to know her.

Her eyes widened, and she stepped closer to him. "Show me," she whispered.

Groaning, he backed her up to the wall, capturing her lips hungrily. Greedily. She had tormented him, brushed him aside, for far too long for him to be gentle. His tongue met hers, stroking as his hands crept up her waist to her bosom.

He traced the line of her cleavage before closing his palms around her, his thumbs toying with her nipples through the thin fabric. Her whimpers urged him on, made him hungry for more. He rubbed his hips against her and groaned. Consuming need took control. The need to claim her. The need to keep her to himself, for always.

"I need you," he whispered.

She nodded, grabbing his hand. Her eyes were a dark blue, stormy and riotous. "Yes. Now."

His heart pounding a rapid staccato in his ears, he let her lead him across the floor, practically dragging him toward the exit. Bloody hell, he wouldn't last more than a minute in bed with her if this continued.

A man stepped in her path. Damon collided with Johanna's back, catching her by the arms before she could hit the floor. Her flush faded to a ghostly pallor.

"Are you okay?" Damon asked.

"The *lady* is fine."

Red hot anger pumped through Damon's veins. Johanna's ex, Tim.

Bloody hell.

"What are you doing here?" Damon snarled. "I'd think rabble like you wouldn't be allowed past security."

"I'm here because I bought a ticket, Sherlock. Too bad

I stopped you two." Tim leaned forward to whisper, "She doesn't often get in the mood."

Red blurred his vision, and Damon snarled, "Get out of our way."

Johanna jerked him back, scowling at Tim. "Don't bother, Damon. He'll leave. He only likes beating on smaller people. Isn't that right, Tim?"

Tim flushed, stepping back to straighten his clothing. "Good luck with her. She's not worth the trouble, I assure you."

"Go to hell, or I'll put you there myself." Damon's fists clenched. He'd love to crush the man into a bloody pulp, but instead focused on his wife. "Are you all right?"

"I'm fi—"

Sauntering past them, Tim strode a few paces away before stopping to glance over his shoulder. "Tell me, Johanna. Do you know where he goes every Sunday? I do."

Johanna froze. "I have an idea, yes."

"Doesn't it bother you that he goes to see her, but doesn't tell you what she is? Who she is?"

Damon couldn't move. Couldn't breathe. How did this… this monster find out about Lilly? How could he know?

Damon would kill him. He wouldn't stop until that foul creature breathed his last. Snarling, he stalked after Tim. Something, or someone, tugged at his elbow.

Snarling, he whirled to face his attacker. Johanna stumbled back from him, eyes wide.

Slowly, the pounding in his skull shrank away, and his fists lowered. Great, he'd managed to give Johanna another reason to mistrust him.

"I'm sorry," he managed. "Let's go to our room."

Striding to her side, he offered his arm with one last look at Tim. Soon, that man would get his full attention. But not here. Not now.

· · ·

Johanna didn't know what to think. Damon had gotten so angry at what Tim said. Obviously this woman he visited held a place in his heart.

And it hurt. Oh, God, did it hurt.

Tears welled in her eyes, blurring her vision. He might still be interested in getting her into bed, but he wouldn't love her. Not like he loved the other woman in his life. If he loved this woman, why had he married Johanna instead of her?

Had he not wanted to start a "real" marriage based on money and contractual obligations? Was Johanna just in the picture so he could continue courting the woman he loved?

And why did it hurt so much to find out that she might mean nothing to him at all?

She entered their suite in silence, Damon following close behind. He sighed, leaning against the door with closed eyes.

"Are you okay?" she asked, taking a hesitant step toward him.

His eyes snapped open, his gaze hard and unrelenting. "No. I'm bloody furious. How *dare* he?"

Damon ripped off his cravat, hurling it across the room with a curse. She retreated. "I'm sorry."

"You should be. He's your bloody ex, not mine," he snapped. He blanched and pressed his lips tightly together. "I'm sorry. I didn't mean it. I'm just upset. Forgive me."

She nodded. Tears spilled down her cheeks. "It's okay."

He shook his head, closing his eyes once more. "No. It's not. Go to bed. I'm not fit company right now."

"Not fit company, or not fit company for me? Who—"

"I said go to bed." His voice was clipped and his lips curled into a snarl.

She nodded, biting her trembling lip. "Fine. I don't enjoy assholes for company, anyway."

She walked to her bedroom and quietly shut the door behind her. What had started out as a dream come true ended up a nightmare.

Johanna crawled into bed and cried herself to sleep.

Chapter Eight

Johanna rolled over in bed, blinking at the sun streaming through the window. She yawned and sat up, rubbing her temples in exhaustion. Sleep had been a long time coming last night. Hell, it had been elusive all week long. The frigid silence she'd been treated to the past few days did nothing to help her rest, and she suspected today would be no different.

Though it was Saturday, she didn't wake up excited. Damon barely spoke to her anymore, so she was pretty sure he wouldn't have a big date planned for the day. With a sigh, she rolled out of bed and trudged down the stairs, entering the dining room with dread. He sat at the table, newspaper in hand.

He glanced up, then turned his attention back to the paper. "Good morning."

"Morning," she mumbled. Crossing the room, she filled a mug with steaming coffee before claiming her seat at his side. Without another word, she pulled her plate close and began eating.

"Tonight I have a charity event to attend. Do you remember me telling you of it the other week?" Damon asked.

She tried to suppress the foolish burst of hope. "Oh. Yeah."

"We shall need to leave by six. You're wearing the dress we spoke of earlier this week, correct?"

"Yes, I am. It's in my room."

He gave her an odd look and rose. "I will see you then. I have some…personal business to attend to."

"Today? But it's not Sunday," she blurted out. *It's my day*.

He raised a brow. "I'm well aware of the day. I'll see you tonight."

She nodded, swallowing heavily. So, now he went to see her on Saturday, too? Then she'd lost the battle for his love before she ever had a chance to win. It was what she wanted, right? To keep her distance and stay safe?

Why, then, did it hurt so much to know she couldn't have him?

The rest of the day passed in a blur of nervous anxiety. Late in the evening, she watched from the bedroom window as he climbed out of the car. Her fingers tightened on the curtain. His stride seemed lighter than before, as if he'd found his pleasure and felt all the better for it.

She shoved away from the window. She couldn't stop picturing the faceless woman hanging all over Damon. He was her husband. He should be happy because of her.

Why couldn't he love her the way she loved him?

Oh. Shit.

Love? Oh, no. Oh, hell no. She couldn't love him…could she? Could she really be so utterly idiotic to fall for a man who didn't love her? To fall for him when he so obviously loved another?

Yes, yes she could.

Son of a bitch.

· · ·

Damon ascended the stairs two at a time. Lilly was safe from Tim; Damon had seen to that. Sure, she'd fought over the relocation, but in the end he'd won. And being able to donate her old house to one of his employees had just been icing on the cake.

It amazed him how much more aware he was of the struggle most people in the world faced. Johanna had opened his eyes, shown him how greedily he had treated life before she came along—without even knowing it. Sure, he went to charity functions occasionally. Donated to good causes.

But now…he actually cared.

He readied himself for the charity event quickly, taking a fast shower before dressing. He opened a drawer to retrieve the box he'd hidden there earlier. Crossing the hallway, he knocked on Johanna's door.

"Come in," she called.

He took a steadying breath and opened the door. "Hey, gorgeous." His gaze fell on the neckline of her low-cut dress. Bloody hell, she would be the death of him. He forced a smile, holding the box behind his back. "You, as usual, look amazing."

"He says with closed eyes."

"They're open." He rocked back on his heels. "I have something for you."

"Oh?" She quirked a brow.

"Yes. Let's try…this?" He held the box out to her, swallowing past his parched throat. "It should match the dress you chose perfectly."

"I'm sure it will," she said dryly, and his stomach sank. "Are you trying to buy my forgiveness for ignoring me all week?"

Damon dragged a hand through his hair. "I wasn't ignoring you. I've just been…busy with work. I'm sorry if you thought I was angry. I didn't mean to give you that impression."

"The last time we really talked, you ordered me to go to my room. What was I supposed to think?"

He sighed. "I know. I'm an ass. Forgive me? Please?"

She gave a slight nod, her face softening a bit, and relief washed over him.

"Thank you. Now, open it."

"Giving me orders again." She hesitantly reached out and took the box. Her hands clutched so tight he could see the whites of her knuckles.

Yet when she opened the box, her breath hitched. Sapphires and diamonds alternated all around the necklace, centered on an enormous sapphire teardrop pendant. "Oh, Damon. You've gone too far. This is way too expensive."

"Nothing is too expensive for you." He coaxed the box out of her hand to remove the necklace from the satin case. Once she saw how gorgeous she looked wearing it, she would not question his motives. The necklace had been made for her.

He draped the jewelry around her neck, and she lifted her hair to accommodate him. He clasped the necklace securely. Unable to resist, he dropped a kiss on her cheek before stepping away. "There. Perfect."

Smiling, she fingered the pendant, studying it in the mirror. "Thank you."

"Don't mention it." Clearing his throat, he tore his gaze from her face. "Ready to go?"

"No. I'm scared," she admitted. "This isn't among Americans. These are your peers. They'll see I'm a fraud."

"Johanna," he groaned, running his hands through his hair. "You'll do great, I promise."

Sighing, she grabbed her purse and brushed past him. "Fine. But I'd rather stay here."

"Me too," he said. "Me too."

• • •

Johanna stared out the car window as traffic flew by. Her stomach cramped as she pictured herself screwing up every single introduction made. Or maybe she'd use the wrong fork—even though she'd been studying the proper order for a week now. Or what if she addressed a Duke as an Earl, or some other such nonsense? Her palms practically slipped off of each other, they were so sweaty. She cringed and wiped them on her jacket.

She looked at Damon. "I can't do this. I'm going to screw this up. I know I am."

He sighed, running his hand through his hair. "No, you're not. This is you we're talking about, not some bumbling amateur. You've been poring over every little detail of the British hierarchy for weeks. You'll do great."

"But what if—"

"Who cares if you mess up? Not I." He reached for her

hand, entwining his fingers with hers. "I don't give a rat's ass what these people think. All I care about is you."

She melted against the seat, closing her eyes. Why did he have to say something so sweet when she was trying to wiggle out of this? "Fine. But don't say I didn't warn you."

The car stopped and Damon got out first, lending her a hand. She tried to ignore her shaking legs. Damon escorted her across the gleaming floor, and her dress swept the hardwood with a soft rustle. Was it her imagination, or did the rustling speed up to match her accelerating heartbeat? The dining hall had been set up elegantly, gold and red tablecloths alternating table by table.

Waiters flitted all around the room while the elite of London society chatted and gossiped. Somewhere in the mix was the Prime Minister. Tonight was all about diplomatic relations with the US, after all, and of course the nobility wouldn't want to miss the party.

Damon squeezed her hand. "You'll be fine. Relax. We're at a party, not an execution."

"I fail to see the difference."

"Ah! Lord and Lady Haymes. How nice of you to come," an elderly gentleman exclaimed, capturing Johanna's hand and bowing over her fingers.

"Good evening, Sir Emerson," Damon said, inclining his head.

Sir. So no curtseying necessary.

She mimicked Damon's nod. "How wonderful to make your acquaintance."

"Ah, you are very lovely, indeed. I've heard all about you."

Johanna blushed. "Thank you, Sir. You are too kind."

"Well, I'll let you go. Wouldn't want to monopolize the

new bride's time. I'm certain everyone wishes to meet her."

The man shuffled away, leaving Damon and Johanna alone. Damon beamed at her. "See? You did excellent."

She eyed the room, wincing. "Yeah. Only ninety more introductions to go."

The rest of the hour passed in a blur of introductions, curtsies, bows, and hand kissing. By the time they were seated at their assigned table, Johanna had a raging headache.

All in all, she'd not messed up anyone's title, and everyone seemed extremely nice. Perhaps unfairly, she'd painted a picture in her head of the gentry that made them out to be snobbish and rude.

A woman sat beside them. Damon tensed. With the woman's every movement, the scent of alcohol assaulted Johanna like some sort of foul perfume. Damon cursed under his breath, and Johanna darted him a surprised glance. The woman caught her eye, watching her with such hatred that Johanna recoiled.

"Oh, Damon, how lovely to see you again. It's been months," the woman simpered.

"Yes, it has," Damon snapped. He gave the woman his shoulder. "So, Johanna, what would you like to have for dinner? Steak, or fish?"

"I was thinking steak," she murmured. Johanna stole another glance at the lady. Yep, the woman despised her. Johanna leaned closer to Damon and whispered, "What's going on?"

"Nothing." He ran a hand over his jaw. His voice was rough. "Are you ready to go? I have a headache."

Johanna blinked. "But—"

"Oh, Damon. Let's not be so childish," the woman said.

"Hi, Johanna. I'm Lady Cecile. Damon's ex-fiancée."

Johanna gasped, digging her fingernails into her palms. Ex-*what*? Her heart ached so badly she thought Damon might have ripped it out right here, for all to see. Was this the woman he left to see every Sunday? Did all his anger stem from the fact that Cecile had confronted him in public and embarrassed him? "Damon?"

Damon clenched his teeth, flushing bright red. "She's not my ex-fiancée. Our courtship never went so far. I thought she might be something along those lines until I caught her in bed under her brother's driver."

Cecile laughed, flashing bright white teeth. Perfect in every way—minus a personality and morals. She defined elegance and grace, but her eyes told a whole other story.

"Oh, who counts servants as infidelity, Damon? Surely you know what I mean, right, Johanna?" Cecile tapped her chin with a scathing look. "Oh, wait. You *are* a servant. How silly of me to forget."

"Knock it off," Damon snarled.

Johanna placed a hand on his shoulder, shooting Cecile a dirty look. Now this was what she'd expected tonight. Johanna could handle Cecile's disdain.

"It's okay, Damon. Some people just don't have any manners."

Cecile glowered, teeth bared. "You have no idea who you're up against."

"We can go home, though, if you'd like," Johanna continued. Holding Damon's hand tightly, she squeezed until his eyes met hers. His expression softened as he focused on her. "Let's go crawl into bed."

His mouth twitched. Standing, he offered her his arm.

"Our obligation is done. I find the dinner company…less than appealing. Shall we?"

Johanna rose, chin held high. "Let's go."

While Damon retrieved their coats and made their excuses, Johanna waited at the door, fuming. How dare that woman insult her at a public dinner, where she couldn't fight back? Bitch.

Heels clinked on the marble floor behind her. Cecile. Digging her fingernails into her palms, Johanna spun to face her with a fake smile.

"Come to finish what you started?"

Cecile stalked closer, smiling snidely. "You know you're nothing but a distraction, right? He'll come to his senses soon enough. Money marries money. Class marries class. You're nothing but a gold-digging American whore."

"Am I?" Johanna asked. "Thanks for letting me know. I had no idea."

"Tell me, peasant. Where does he go every Sunday?" Cecile whispered, eyes gleaming.

Johanna flinched inwardly, but attempted to remain calm. "You? Really?"

Cecile hesitated, her smile faltering, then smoothing over again. "Yes. Me."

"I can't believe it," Johanna whispered.

"He'll divorce you soon, and come running back to me. Men like him don't stay with women like you." Her eyes flashed and she dug her nails into Johanna's bare arm, squeezing hard. When she spoke, Johanna recoiled from the stench of booze on her breath. "We laugh at men who marry beneath their status in life. Call them stupid and foolhardy. You're nothing more to him than a whore!"

Something inside of her snapped. She jerked her arm free, advancing on the "lady." "He didn't marry me because he loves me, you idiot. It's an arrangement. Nothing more than a business transaction. If he runs back to you after we're through with our contract, I pity him. Hell, he can even bang you now, for all I care. I don't love him, so you won't break my heart."

She spun on her heel to retreat, but ran into a solid chest instead. Damon glowered down at her, jaw tight. Shame churned in her gut, her stomach turning until she thought she might throw up. His searching stare turned hard—cold.

Cecile's eyes glowed in triumph. "I knew it."

Johanna shook her head, swallowing past the lump in her throat. She couldn't talk, or she'd shame herself by crying in front of the bitch. Damn it.

"Cecile? Go to hell." Damon grabbed Johanna's hand, dragging her outside. When they reached the car, Damon ushered her in before slouching down beside her.

Johanna closed her eyes, fighting for control. Why had she allowed Cecile to get to her? Why would she let her temper out to play? She knew better. Worse, she knew Cecile was right.

Soon, whether at the end of the year or before, Damon would realize she wasn't good enough for him. He'd move on with his life and his money. She'd become the forgotten ex-wife he'd married to save his fortune. Maybe he'd occasionally remember her with fondness. But nothing more.

While Johanna?

Johanna was the idiot who'd gone and fallen in love with him.

Chapter Nine

Damon watched the hotel in the rearview mirror, glowering at Cecile's condescending smile. He itched to wrap his hands around her scrawny little throat. How dare she accost his wife?

And therein lay the other problem. His wife.

The past few weeks, he'd allowed himself to think maybe she would come to care for him, even just a little bit.

But tonight, she'd let him know loud and clear that he would only ever be her business partner, and she'd have no problem walking away from him.

He couldn't blame her. He'd never asked her to love him…or even to like him. Why, then, did he shake from the need to scream? Why had she ripped his heart out and cut it into tiny pieces?

Hand unsteady, he ran his fingers through his hair while covertly studying her. At his movement, she faced him, her eyes glimmering with unshed tears.

Shit.

"I'm sorry I lost my temper. Embarrassing you isn't something I'm supposed to do as your—" She thumped her fist on her thigh. "—wife."

"I never asked you to be perfect," he snapped. He couldn't help himself. She'd *hurt* him. "It isn't in the contract."

She flinched, looked down at her hands, and sighed. He fought the urge to wrap his arm around her shoulder and comfort her. He needed to distance himself from her. He'd gotten too close. Too fast.

"I know. But still, I'm sorry for embarrassing you."

Her voice sounded like she might be crying, and he clenched his jaw. He bit his tongue. Didn't she know she apologized for the wrong bloody thing? She should be apologizing for breaking his heart, not for yelling at a bitch who deserved everything she'd gotten. Control. He needed control.

"Don't mention it. I'm fine," he managed.

Tears ran down her face. "No, you're not. You're mad at me."

No, I'm not bloody mad at you. I'm mad at me. "No. I'm just tired. I have a headache, remember?"

The car pulled in front of the house, and she shook her head. "You're not being honest. I can feel it."

Honest? She wanted honesty? "Fine," he spat. The car door opened, and he yanked it shut. "I'm pissed because you told her about our arrangement. I'm pissed you told her she could have me. I'm even more pissed I let your words matter to me so much."

She reached out to grab his hand. He jerked away.

"I didn't mean—"

"I don't need to hear your apologies. You're right. We have a business arrangement. Nothing more."

She swallowed heavily, nodding. "Right. Just like we said."

"Now, can you go inside? I find myself in the mood for a drink."

"We have wine inside. I can grab the bottle," she said, reaching for the door handle.

"No. I'm going out for a little while. Alone."

A flash of pain crossed over her eyes and then disappeared. He stared her down, steeling his heart against the surprised look on her face. He didn't need to make her feel better. Didn't need to apologize for being blunt. It wasn't in the contract.

"So, if you'd please get out?" he ground through his teeth.

"Oh." Shoulders stiff, she exited the car and fled into the house.

He watched the door close behind her and kicked the seat in front of him. *I don't love him, so you won't break my heart.* Of course she didn't love him. She didn't give a damn about him. His plan to make a serious go of their marriage was crumbling.

The driver opened to door. "My lord?"

"Take me to a strip club. Any strip club."

"Yes, my lord," the man said after a slight hesitation.

"Wait."

The driver stopped. "Yes?"

"Make it a bar instead."

Son of a bitch. Even now, when he wanted to hate her with all of his heart, she controlled him. He was nothing but her puppet—and she didn't even know her own power.

. . .

Johanna marched up the stairs and shut the door to her room before she allowed herself to burst into sobs and collapse onto the bed. What a fool she'd been. For a minute, she'd thought he might have cared about her, but his reminder of her "status" as his business partner ruined all of those silly notions.

She was the only confused idiot in this business-only marriage. Undressing, she crawled onto the bed in only her slip. Damon probably wouldn't be coming home tonight. More than likely, he was on his way to Cecile's even now.

Wrapping her arms around herself, she closed her eyes tightly and tried not to imagine where he might be right now.

At some point, she must have drifted off to sleep, for she lurched awake with a gasp. Sweat crept down her spine as she stood up and walked to the window, just in time to see the car pull up. She dropped the curtains as if they were on fire and jerked back from the pane. Her eyes watered and she straightened her spine. He might be her spouse by law, but he wasn't her husband. He didn't love her.

And she wouldn't cry over him anymore.

The door opened and she jumped. Damon entered her room, hair disheveled and cheeks flushed. The tie he'd been wearing earlier now rested in his hand, and he'd unbuttoned his shirt. His eyes fell on her, cold and hard.

"Oh, look. It's my wife." He stumbled inside the room, scowling as he worked his way toward her. He said the word *wife* like it was a curse. "Did you wait up for me? How…

nice."

"This is my room, Damon. You entered the wrong room," she pointed out.

"No. I came to the right room."

She tensed, tossing her hair over her shoulder. He reeked of booze and perfume. "You woke me up."

He eyed her skeptically, looking from the watch in her hand to her face. "Now who isn't being honest?"

She flinched. "Fine. I woke up and saw you weren't home. I was checking the time."

"Ah. The truth comes out," he said as he stalked closer. She skirted past him, heading toward the door. She had no desire to see him like this. "Hey. Where are you going?"

"Your room. We'll talk in the morning." She closed her hand around the knob.

"Wait!" He stumbled after her. "Don't go. Please."

She closed her eyes. He'd been out with *Cecile*—and he wanted her to crawl into his arms? Not likely. "I have to."

"I'm not drunk. I tried to get drunk, but the drinks weren't working tonight." He pulled her into his arms. "I need you beside me."

She bit her lip. "You didn't seem to mind leaving me before."

"I was mad. Hurt. I'm better now, see?" He kissed her forehead.

"I didn't mean to hurt you," she whispered.

"I know." His heart raced underneath her cheek. "Can I stay?"

Did she have a choice? "Okay."

She crawled into bed, holding her breath as he stepped out of his pants. "Where did you go?"

He tensed, pants halfway down his legs. "A bar."

She swallowed heavily. "Did you…" *Go screw Cecile?* "…meet anyone new?"

"No. I don't want to meet anyone. Or sleep with anyone. Or even look at another woman." He crawled into bed, pulling her against his chest. "I only want you."

"You must be drunk," she mumbled. "Stop it, Damon."

"I'm not bloody drunk. I'm just sick of lying. Sick of pretending to not care when I do."

"Damon…" She struggled to break free of his hold. "You don't even know what you're saying. Go to sleep. We'll talk in the morning."

"I know damn well what I'm saying, Johanna. I love you. There. I said it. I love you."

"No, you don't!" Tears burned her eyes and rolled down her cheeks. No, he didn't love her. Couldn't love her. He'd leave her, just like her parents had. It was only a matter of time.

"I do, Johanna." He kissed her cheek, his breath fanning over her face. His breath smelled sweet. Not like alcohol. Was he sober? She spread her palms over his chest. Should she push him away…or pull him closer?

"Damon," she whispered, her voice cracking.

"Johanna, let me love you. Let me show you how much I love you," he whispered, kissing her. He slid atop her, his skin pressing against hers in tantalizing temptation. His eyes burned into hers, crystal clear and not the slightest bit foggy from alcohol.

"And if I tell you to go?"

"I'll leave. Do you doubt I'd honor my word?" His grip tightened on her shoulders. "I would never force my attentions on you."

"I know. You're an honorable man."

"Mmhm." He nuzzled her neck. His fingers caressed her shoulders. "I have to warn you, though. I'm feeling less than honorable right now."

"I don't want you to be honorable," she whispered. "Not anymore."

"Thank God," he breathed. He melded his mouth to hers, stroking her tongue with his own. She whimpered, pressing closer. His breathing matched hers, hot and heavy, as he lifted himself over her. He met her eyes, cheeks flushed. "Are you certain? Last chance to back down."

"Kiss me." She tangled her fingers in his hair, arching to press against him. He let out a tortured groan, his hands roving over her body. Her breasts, her hips, her thighs. Everywhere he touched, she burned. Her body begged for more. Squirming, she tugged at his shirt, aching to feel his skin against hers.

He tore his shirt over his head before kissing a path down her neck to the top of her chemise. She whimpered, running her nails over his back. When his lips closed over her nipple through the sheer fabric, she cried out and arched her hips. Her body went crazy, trembling with need. Her fingers dug into his skin, desperate to hold onto him. To feel him with her.

He rubbed against her, moaning. Lifting her gown, he stroked the fabric over her thighs until she lay bare. His heated gaze roamed over her, leaving her feeling exposed and beautiful. He kissed her until she forgot to breathe. Lightheaded, she grabbed his hips, pulling him close. "Now."

"Johanna," he groaned, positioning himself at her

entrance. "I love you."

He kissed her poignantly before thrusting inside. He filled her completely, leaving her shivering and yet oh so hot. Lifting her hips, she met his thrust, trailing her fingers over his chest. He groaned, arching his neck back.

"Oh God," he cried out, increasing his tempo. An answering hunger rose in her, making her writhe beneath him. He reached between them, caressing her until she lost all control. After a few quick movements of his thumb, stars burst in front of her eyes as pleasure consumed her. He collapsed on top of her, lips pressed into the side of her neck.

"I can't imagine my life without you," he breathed.

She closed her eyes, savoring his embrace and the relief washing over her. His breath feathered her hair, tickling her forehead. Maybe she should tell him she cared about him. Maybe she should let him know the truth.

"Damon?"

His snore echoed through the room. He'd fallen asleep.

• • •

The next day, Damon sat at his desk. He rubbed his forehead and let out a groan. For the second time in his life, he'd allowed himself to be driven to drink over a woman who didn't even want him. The worst part was that it hadn't worked. He'd still been absolutely miserable. No. Scratch that. He'd been *drunk* and miserable. But by the time he'd gotten home, he'd been completely sober. And then he'd somehow managed to make his dreams come true. He'd spent the night wrapped in her embrace.

But now what?

He'd, like a bloody fool, confessed his love to her, practically begging for a scrap of affection, and she said nothing in return. Even after they made love, she'd remained silent. He didn't know what to think. Had they made love because she returned his feelings—or did it mean nothing more to her than a pity fuck?

What was going through her head? What was she feeling? He was terrified to find out. If she came downstairs as if she hadn't a care in the world and nothing ever happened between them, he might explode. This was not a game to him. He couldn't shrug off her disinterest as he would any other woman. Johanna was different.

If he lost her…he'd have nothing left.

• • •

"…So we need to call them by three tomorrow."

Damon blinked, eyeing Jeff. "Call who?"

Jeff rolled his eyes. "I've told you four times already. What's your problem today? Did Johanna keep you up too late?"

"Tell me again. I'll listen."

Jeff gave him an odd look. A knock sounded, and the butler opened the door a crack. "My lord? There's a Mr. Smith here to see you. Shall I show him in?"

"Absolutely not." Damon snarled, rising to his feet. "You can tell him to go straight to he—"

"No thanks," Tim answered as he shoved past the butler. "I need to speak to him. Alone."

Damon nodded and arched a brow, crossing his arms over his chest. Once Jeff left the room, he turned his attention back to Tim.

"What do you want?"

Tim sauntered close, his eyes flitting around the room as if taking a tally of Damon's possessions. "I was wondering how things were going between you and the cold little witch. Have you gotten her into your bed yet?"

Damon clenched his fists, picturing the man with his face smashed in. It would feel so damn good to be the one doing the smashing. "Get the hell out of my house."

He shook his head. "Did you think that if you moved her, I wouldn't know?"

Damon's head spun. Lilly. What the hell did this bastard want from him? "Yes," he said. "Why do you care about her? Why are you doing this?"

"I have my reasons. Why did you have to marry Johanna? We planned everything so well."

Damon gritted his teeth. "We?"

"How's Lilly's new place?" Tim rubbed his chin, lounging against the wall. "I like the flowers out front."

Damon reached the end of his limited patience. "You stay away from her. And Johanna."

"Johanna is a whore. This whole plan fell apart because of you marrying her. Did you fuck her yet?"

That was it. This sick game was over. Damon advanced on Tim—until he caught a flash of something blue in the doorway, and froze.

Johanna, face pale and eyes wide, stood in the open office door, Jeff behind her. Tim smirked as Damon rushed forward.

"Johanna."

"Don't bother. I'm leaving now," Johanna said, her voice

breaking on the last word. "Let me know when you two decide who gets custody of me."

"As if I'd want you," Tim called out. "He called me here, asking me if I knew where your family is so he could send you off to them. He can't stand being married to a useless whore like you."

"Shut up," Damon snarled, shoving the man backward. "Jeff, if you don't get him out of here right now, I will be going to jail for murder."

"I'll take care of it. You go get your wife back," Jeff said.

Damon entered the foyer, only to catch a glimpse of her disappearing up the stairs at a run. "Johanna!" he cried. Damon bolted after her, heart thumping at crazy speeds in his chest. "Stop right now."

Her shoulders squared off as she whirled to face him. Her eyes were icy and cold—emotionless. Her lips trembled, but otherwise she looked completely under control. "Is that an order?"

"Of course it's not a bloody order," he spat, skidding to a halt at her side. "What's wrong with you?"

"I heard you two talking about me. Tell me the truth. What's going on?"

"The truth?" he echoed, rubbing his neck. "I have no bloody idea what you're talking about. That's the truth."

"Is this all a setup? Planned by him to make me look like a fool?"

Damon threw his hands up in the air. "Are you insane? I never even met the man until I met you. Why would I agree to some sort of sick agreement with your ex?"

"You tell me!" she shouted, face red. "I knew you couldn't be the real thing. You're nothing but a liar. And I slept with you!"

Fury pounded in his head. He clenched his fists tightly. He needed to stay calm. In control. "Why are you doing this to us? Why are you pushing me away?"

She held herself, rocking slightly. "There is no us. There never was. This thing we call a marriage? It isn't right." She wrung her hands. "Can't you see we're not good for each other?"

"You've not given me a chance to be good for you." He ran a hand over his jaw. "You won't let me near you. Why? Do you hate me so much?"

"Hate you? I don't hate you. I've never hated you," she whispered.

"Then why are you refusing to let me love you? Why are you making crazy accusations to push me away?"

"You need a real wife! One who will love you back." Her jaw tightened.

"Why won't you bloody listen to me? I want you. Not someone else," he insisted. Desperation clawed at his chest. He couldn't breathe. He could really lose her right now, if he couldn't convince her to believe in him.

She shook her head. "You can't have me. I'm not yours to keep."

His hands dropped to his side, numb. The fight drained from him. "You'll never believe I love you, will you? I can't make you see what's right in front of your face."

"No. You can't fix me. I'm not a charity project. I'm real. And I can't love you. I'm sorry."

He glanced out the bedroom window. He couldn't even stand to look at her right now. Her cold face staring back at him; her bitter heart crushing his. "Did you ever care about me? Or is this all a game to you?"

"I did what I had to do."

"That's not what I asked," he snapped.

"I can't answer." She shook her head frantically. "Don't make me."

"Coward," he said. "I'm beginning to wish that I'd never bid on you on Valentine's Day. None of this was worth it."

He spun on his heel, stomping down the stairs and straight into his office. He closed the door, leaning against the wood. Johanna's papers rested on the table, covered in glue and obnoxious amounts of sparkles. Even here, in his sanctuary, he couldn't escape her.

Blood pumped in his ears as he charged toward his desk. Roaring, he shoved everything off of it, sending his business papers flying. Not satisfied, he picked up a chair and chucked it against the wall. It crashed into pieces.

Footsteps pounded overhead. Probably Johanna. She'd be wondering at the noise, no doubt. He couldn't stand for her to see him like this—broken, angry, and bitter.

The last thing he needed was Johanna knowing how much he was hurt right now. He glowered at her papers— untouched and still sparkling merrily—and stormed out of the room, past a pale Jeff, and out into the snow. Screw it. He didn't need to suffer through this. Didn't need to torture himself any longer.

He was going home.

• • •

Johanna wandered down the stairs and cringed. Two ser-vants were carrying out bits and pieces of what appeared to have once been a chair, while another cleaned up broken glass with a broom. A mournful silence covered the whole house, bearing down oppressively. The butler overlooked the cleaning crew, his lips pinched tightly. She tapped him on the shoulder.

He met her eyes, then he reached into his pocket. "I have a letter for you, my lady."

"Johanna," she reminded him. "Thank you."

She took the letter and tore it open. Could it be a letter from Damon? No; the writing didn't match up. Her world titled beneath her feet with each word she read. How could this be happening? And why now, of all times?

"Are you well, my lady?" the butler inquired. He grabbed her elbow to steady her.

"Yes. Yes, I'm fine. I'm sorry. Do you know when Damon will be back?" she asked.

The butler dropped his gaze to his feet and cleared his throat. "He didn't say, my lady."

"Johanna," she corrected absently. Where was Damon? She really needed to talk to him about what they had said—and his reaction to it. "Where did he go?"

"Er, he booked a flight to London."

"London?" she whispered. "He's gone to London?"

Numbness spread over her body, leaving her weak. She felt like a fist had reached into her chest, squeezing until there was no feeling left for her to spare.

The butler flushed. "Yes, London."

"I see."

Her feet felt weighed by iron as she backed away, then fled. She wouldn't stay here. Couldn't be in this house that wasn't hers and never would be. How could she remain in this sham of a marriage when it only proved what she'd known all along? No one could be trusted—not even him. He'd left her. Right in the moment when she needed him most.

Wait. Since when did she need him—or anyone, for that matter? She'd always done fine on her own. Been fine on her own. All she ever needed was people like Sara. Someone she could laugh with on her lunch break, but who didn't get involved in her personal life. No true friends. No confidantes. Certainly not lovers.

And certainly not Damon.

So why did it hurt so much to know he'd left, when she'd done everything she could to push him away?

Because she did need him. More than anything. Johanna pressed her knuckles to her mouth. She was a fool. A self-absorbed, cowardly fool who'd hurt the one person who'd proven he would stand by her, no matter what. She couldn't do this alone. Couldn't handle life without him, but it was too late.

She'd pushed him away, and he'd left her for good.

Chapter Ten

Damon stood outside the house, bracing himself for the coming confrontation. It might have only been a few days since he'd left, but it felt more like a lifetime.

Entering the house, he strode past his shocked butler, heading straight into his library. Someone had cleaned up, fixing the demolition he'd left in his wake.

Jeff stood, eyes wide. "You're back? That was fast."

"What are you doing here?" Damon asked.

"I'm looking for the file on May's shipment for the accountant." Jeff came around the desk and clapped Damon on the shoulder. "Welcome home."

"Thanks. Where's Johanna?"

Jeff's gaze slid to the floor. "Uh, look. There's something I have to tell you."

"Can it wait?" Damon headed for the door. "I'm looking for Johanna."

As he passed the table where she often sat, he saw the

papers she'd been marking still sat there — over a week old. Dread crept into his mind and refused to leave. Why would those papers still be on the table?

"It's about her," Jeff said quietly. "She's gone."

Damon froze, his gut wrenching painfully. "Gone? Gone, where?"

"No one knows. She left the day after you." Jeff came to his side, handing him a tumbler of whiskey. "I'm sorry."

"Gone," Damon repeated. He handed the glass back to Jeff. "I'll go to the school in the morning and see her there, then. Once I explain — "

"She quit." Jeff shoved the glass into Damon's hands and backed away. "When I say she's gone…I mean completely."

Damon sank into the nearest chair, misery squeezing the air out of his chest until he wondered if this was how he would die, heartbroken and abandoned. "She left me."

"Well…you did leave first."

"No, I didn't." Damon snapped. Then…oh, then it hit him. He'd *left*. After all the things she told him about her past, after all her fears…he'd left her. Bloody hell, he had done this. He'd pushed her away by abandoning her. By rousing all the fears she'd tried to lay to rest because he had to be a cold, callous idiot and retreat.

How could he be such a fool? How could he forget, for even the slightest second, that she would be devastated? Betrayed? She wouldn't see it for what it really meant: a time out. She would assume he'd left her for good, just like everyone else in her life.

Shit, shit, shit.

"I need to find her, Jeff." He met his friend's gaze, determination straightening his spine. He rose to his feet, narrowing his eyes. "I *will* find her."

. . .

Damon stared at the red light, hands tightening on the steering wheel. A week. A whole useless, sleepless week searching, and still no trace of Johanna. He'd stalked the school parking lot so often the principal had threatened to call the police. Still he went.

If anyone knew where Johanna was, it would be Sara. He'd begged, cajoled, and pleaded for any scrap of information, but she'd sworn she didn't know. She was probably lying.

But if he didn't find Johanna, and soon, he didn't know what he'd do. When his house came into view, a groan dragged out of him. The familiar thrill of coming home was gone. Johanna had taken it with her. He dragged himself out of the car, but walking seemed to take too much effort.

The *clack* of a woman's heels echoed as he entered the foyer. He stopped, for a split second frozen by euphoria.

She came back. His Johanna was back.

Gripping the banister, he whirled to face her. When she rounded the corner, he took an eager step in her direction, only to freeze mid-stride.

It wasn't Johanna. It was *her*.

"Why are you here?" he snarled.

Cecile smiled, sashaying to his side. "I heard she left you."

Damon tensed. "Oh? Where did you hear that?"

"A friend." She waved her hand. "Who cares? He's not important. What is important is the fact that you need a wife."

"I have a wife," he growled. "Get out."

"Not anymore you don't. You need a wife in this house with you, or you'll lose everything."

Damon shrugged "I don't give a damn."

"Are you insane?" She gripped his shoulder. "You need your money. You can't let it go to waste."

He laughed, rubbing the back of his neck. "Honestly? I really don't care."

"You've gone mad." She stared at him.

"No. For the first time ever, I'm seeing clearly. I don't need to be rich to be happy. I just need her."

"You're a fool," she spat, shaking him. "She left you and ran all the way across the country...and you want her back? After she abandoned you and cursed you to a life of poverty?"

"I won't give up. I'll find her someday and—" He broke off. "How do you know where she is?"

"What?" She blanched. "I-I don't."

"You lie." He gripped her shoulders. "Tell me, and tell me now, or I'll call your parents. I'll let them know you've been sleeping with every servant you can get your hands on, and you're drinking again. I'm sure they'd love to hear the truth about their darling daughter. In fact, I'd wager they'd send you straight back to rehab—and cut off your stipend."

"They won't believe you!" she cried.

"Won't they?"

She trembled in his arms. "Fine. Have it your way. Your slut is in California."

"California?" He shook his head. "Why the hell would she go out there?"

"She got a letter from her father. Or..." Cecile shrugged free of his grip. "She thought she did."

"Get out," he snapped. "And pray that I never see you again."

Her heels *clack*ed on the floor in rapid tempo as she fled.

...

Johanna lay on the hotel bed, torn between bawling her eyes out and vomiting. Maybe both. Why in the world would anyone do this? What kind of sicko would fake a letter asking her to bail her father out of jail?

And why didn't it hurt more?

She missed Damon. Had he come back yet? Did he even know she'd left? Would he care? She couldn't bring herself to call and find out. Couldn't make herself dial the number to the house. What if he answered? Worse, what if he hung up on her?

And what about the children and the charity? If she left he'd lose all his money, and no one would benefit from this mess. Well, no one except the distant cousin in France.

But how could she stay? Could she bear being near him, yet unable to have his love? Could she handle his scorn? She had to. The children needed that money worse than she needed her freedom. But being with him just might end up killing her. She loved the bastard. And he'd walked away. Had he left because of their fight, or had he given up on her? Did she even want to know?

She grabbed her phone, running her thumb lightly over the keypad. Her eyes burned as she sat up. She glanced down at the unopened box on the bed, toying with it. Maybe she should go to the bathroom first. Then call. No, call first. Then bathroom. Maybe. Damn it. She liked her world neatly ordered, but there was nothing neat about this.

A knock sounded at the door, and she stood up. Her stomach growled. Room service, she hoped. She could already taste the cheeseburger she'd ordered.

"Come in, I'll grab my wallet," she said, smiling at the man in the hallway—until she realized it wasn't room service at all.

It was Damon.

Stumbling back, she pressed a shaky hand to her mouth. He took advantage of the opportunity to enter the room, shutting the door behind him.

"Hello, wife." He held a yellow manila envelope in his hand, which he chucked onto the bed. In his other hand he held her dinner, which he set down on the table. "Did you miss me?"

"H-how did you find me?" Swallowing past the huge lump in her throat, she took a step closer to him. Her arms ached with the need to wrap around him. "Why are you here?"

"Do you know how many bloody hotels there are in this city? Jesus, I thought I would never find you."

She shook her head and searched his face, greedily drinking in the sight of him. "How did you find me here?"

"A lot of driving, calling, begging, pleading, and a little bit of bribery." He gave her a half smile and ran his hand over his face. He gave her a weary smile, and her legs threatened to crumble beneath her. God, she'd missed him. His gaze moved over her, taking in every detail.

She suddenly wished she'd worn something sexier than

shorts and a tank top.

"I brought papers for you," he said. His face closed off. "You look tired."

She smoothed her free hand over her hair, grimacing. "I am."

"I missed you," he whispered, and her stomach clenched. "A lot."

"I missed you, too." Tears ran down her cheeks, but she ignored them. They didn't matter. Not now. "What's in the envelope?"

He strode to the bed, opening the manila folder. "Divorce papers."

She gasped. "B-but…" Her mind raced. "Your money. You'll lose it all."

"I know. And I don't care." His eyes never left hers.

"What?"

"All I want is you. I love you, and I'm sorry I left."

Her vision blurred. "But you left me when I needed you. How could you do that? My father—the note—"

"I didn't know about the note until after I came back. Cecile sent it to hurt you. To separate us." He flinched. "I suppose she didn't need to. I didn't think it through when I left. I just wanted some space to think. I wasn't leaving you. Not really."

"You could have called. Something. God, if I'd known Cecile had—" She broke off.

He leaned closer. "What? What if you'd known?"

Something in his eyes compelled her to be honest. "…I would have waited for you."

"Why didn't you wait for me? Call me? Even a letter." He touched her cheek. "Johanna, haven't I earned even a sliver of your trust?"

"You have." Her throat ached. "It's not your fault. I just...I assumed you were done with me. Done with us."

He gripped her shoulders, stroking the bare skin with his thumbs. "I wasn't abandoning you. I panicked and ran. It was stupid, but I don't want to lose you."

"Then why are you divorcing me?"

"Because I love you. You're right," he said. "We never should have gotten married like we did. I thought I needed the money to survive. I thought I needed it to keep Lilly safe. But I know now there are worse things in life than being poor."

She frowned. "Hold up, right now. If we're going to be a real couple, you will tell me once and for all. Who the hell is Lilly? I thought you were going to see Cecile on Sundays."

"Cecile? Hell no. Why would I visit her?" He threw a frustrated glance at the ceiling. "I'm trying to pour out my love to you, and all you care about is my sister and my ex?"

"Sister?" she squeaked. "You have a sister?"

"Yes," he answered slowly. "I thought you knew. You told Tim that you knew where I went every Sunday."

Relief washed over her. "Oh. So that's where you were? Not with a lover?"

"A lover? Are you insane?" he ground out. "When did I ever give you the impression that I had a lover? Or wanted one, besides you?"

"Well, you left every Sunday, not telling me where you went. What else was I supposed to think?"

"Bloody hell." He slapped his forehead. "I didn't think of it like that. I just didn't want you to meet her if—if you weren't staying in my life. She gets attached to people."

"Why?" she asked.

"She has special needs. And when she meets someone she likes, she won't let him or her out of her sight. If she meets you, she'll love you. How could she not?"

Johanna melted, and her face went hot. Just when she thought he couldn't be any sweeter, he went and proved her wrong. "Where does she live?"

"About ten minutes from us. She likes to live on her own, so I have her set up in a house with servants. She always wanted to see America...so I brought her." He shrugged. His lips curled into a smile. "I've tried to get her to live with me endless times, but she refuses. She says she enjoys her freedom far too much to live with a man."

Johanna laughed. "Smart woman. I like her already."

Damon sobered. "Sign these, and you're free. Sign these, and we can start over again. I already signed on the dotted line. It only waits for you."

"No. I'm not signing."

Damon dragged a hand through his hair. "It's for the best. We need a new start. I'll get an accounting job to take care of Lilly, and you can keep teaching."

Shaking her head, she bit her lip. "No. I'm not letting you lose it all to prove a point."

"But I don't care about any of it. I don't want it. It's done nothing but cause trouble."

"We can change that," she assured him. "We will. But, I'm not divorcing you. Not now. Not ever."

He cleared his throat. His face flushed and his lips twitched upward. "Does that mean that you love me?"

"I love you," she answered with a smile.

Whooping, he captured her in his arms and spun her

about. Her empty stomach lurched in protest. Oh, God. Not now.

"I love you, too," he murmured. He kissed her hard, his fingers threading in her hair.

She jerked out of his arms, bolting for the bathroom. She barely made it to the toilet before her stomach revolted, emptying itself completely. He crouched beside her, holding her hair back while she retched. When she finished, she flushed the toilet and lay back against the tub.

Damon wet a washcloth and handed it to her, eyebrow raised. "Is my kiss that revolting?"

"Go get the box off of the bed in the other room," she murmured, burying her face in the warm terrycloth.

"What box?"

"You'll know when you see it," she mumbled, shooing him away with one hand.

He reentered moments later, carrying a pink box. His eyes were wide, his face pale. "Are you…are you pregnant?"

She shot him a look, rolling her eyes. "I don't know. I asked, but the box didn't answer me yet."

He chuckled, tearing it open enthusiastically. "Well, go on."

She eyed him and took the foil wrapped stick from his fingers. "No offense, but get out. I'm not peeing in front of you."

He opened his mouth—and promptly shut it when she glared at him. With a foolish grin, he strode out and shut the door behind him. She pulled herself to her feet.

"Are you done yet? What does it say?" he called through the door.

Closing her eyes and praying for patience, she answered,

"I haven't even gotten my shorts off yet. Relax."

"Right. Sorry," he mumbled. His footsteps paced back and forth outside the door.

Shaking her head and laughing, she got down to business, only calling him in once she was decently covered and the toilet flushed. Her heartbeat pounded in her ears as she studied the white window on the test. They both hovered over the stick. He sighed impatiently.

"Calm down," she hissed.

"There are two lines!" he shouted, holding the box up in her face. "See? It says if there are two lines—"

"That I'm pregnant," she finished, smiling. Her hands drifted down to her stomach. "I'm pregnant."

"We're having a baby," he said with wonder. Picking her up, he hugged her tightly and buried his face in her neck. He kissed her reverently, as if she would break if he held her too hard.

He carried her into the bedroom, setting her down next to her food. "Feed our baby," he commanded, grinning from ear to ear. "Wait until we tell Lilly. She'll flip."

"Does she like babies?"

"Oh, yeah. Loves them."

Johanna grinned. She suspected she and Lilly would get along splendidly. "I can't wait to meet her."

"And I can't wait for her to meet you." He sat down next to her. "Just don't go comparing stories behind my back. That never turns out well."

"Would I do such a thing?"

He groaned and flopped onto his back. "Yes. I do believe you would."

His forlorn expression was too much to resist. "Don't

worry. I'll still love you if I find out you wet the bed until you were thirteen."

He choked on a laugh. "Oh dear God. What have I done? You'll kill me yet."

She shot him a heated glance. "I'll be gentle…most of the time."

His tortured groan filled the silence. "Yes. I'm a dead man."

. . .

After she finished eating, Damon pulled her into his arms, cradling her close.

"I love you, Johanna," he whispered, kissing her tentatively.

"I love you, too." She tugged him closer, sealing her mouth to his.

He pulled away, gasping for air. "Maybe we should take it easy. I don't want to hurt you."

"You won't. I'm pregnant, not dead." She stroked his jaw.

He kissed her, caressing the side of her breast. Her heart faltered as she returned his kiss, her tongue gliding against his. He moaned, pulling her on top of him until she straddled his hips. She rotated her hips, teasing him. He broke free of the kiss, ripping her tank top over her head and tossing it across the room. His gaze fell on her bare breasts, darkening with desire.

"God, you're perfect," he said and closed his lips around her nipple. She arched her back, whimpering. His hand massaged her other breast as he tortured her with his tongue and teeth, making her tremble for more.

He rolled her onto her back and tore her shorts off, undressing himself once she was naked. He kissed his way up her leg, finding her core and driving her insane with his tongue. He didn't stop until she exploded with pleasure, the world freezing around her. Then, with a tormented growl, he plunged into her, throwing his head back when he entered her completely. She dug her fingers into his back as he brought her higher and higher, claiming her as his in every way. When he found his pleasure, she cried out, joining him.

They lay together, spent, wrapped in each other's arms. Their limbs tangled so thoroughly she could scarcely tell where he stopped and she began. Sighing in contentment, she traced a pattern on his chest. His hand rested on her stomach.

"Do you want a boy or a girl?" she asked.

"I don't care. I'll be happy with either." His voice rumbled in her ear. "You?"

"The same," she answered. "We should wait to find out until we have the baby. Let it be a surprise."

He groaned. "No way. I need to know."

She laughed. "You will…when it comes out."

"Or when we go to the ultrasound," he responded, tapping her nose.

"Or when it comes out."

He laughed, kissing her into silence.

Chapter Eleven

Damon entered their house with a sense of completeness, unable to hold back his smile. They were home. Happy. In love. Could things get any better?

He yanked Johanna into his arms, kissing her senseless. She clung to his shoulders, pressing her delicious body against his. Moaning low in his throat, he deepened the kiss, his hands creeping down her back.

"Ahem," Jeff said from the office. Johanna jumped out of Damon's embrace, flushing. "I'm glad to see you two looking so cozy, but you might want to come in here."

"No offense, but no thank you." Grabbing Johanna's hand, Damon tugged her toward the stairs.

Chuckling, she followed without hesitation. "Sorry. Gotta agree with the husband on this one."

Jeff sighed, rolling his eyes. "Fine. I'll tell the fake lawyer in the library to wait until you're done having sex, then."

Damon froze. "Fake lawyer?"

"Yes," Jeff answered, examining his fingernails. "But, hey. You two go ahead. Have fun."

Damon growled, heading down the stairs with Johanna in tow. "Jeff, don't piss me off. You know how that ends."

Jeff snorted. "Yeah, with my foot up your—"

"Jeff!" he growled. Jeff entered the library, followed closely by Johanna and Damon. Damon's head raced when he saw the scrawny man who had crashed into his life and changed everything. "You? You're a fraud?"

"That's what he says," Jeff answered. "But he'll tell you the rest."

"Speak," Damon commanded, motioning for Johanna to sit. She sank into a nearby chair, biting her lip. "And be quick."

The man cleared his throat, blanching at the sight of Damon. "Your father's will never stated you must marry. My employer threatened my family's safety and forced me to falsify the documents and come to you, telling you of the clause so you would have to marry her. Now that she's fled back to England, I can tell you the truth."

All the puzzle pieces snapped into place, and Damon groaned. "Let me guess. Your employer is Cecile."

The man nodded enthusiastically. "Yes. And her cousin, a Mr. Smith."

Johanna sat upright, gasping. "Tim Smith?"

"Yes, my lady," Mr. Johnson responded, bowing his head. "They have both fled the continent, and I told the police. They're searching for them even now."

"Bloody hell," Damon murmured, sitting next to Johanna and capturing her hand. "So is that how Tim knew about Lilly?"

"Yes, my lord. I heard her tell him," Mr. Johnson said.

Damon shook his head, then looked at Johanna. "Can you believe this?"

She laughed, shaking her head. "Not really."

After an incredulous moment, laughter overwhelmed him.

The "lawyer" cleared his throat. "I'm sorry, my lord, for my part in their scheme. I wanted to be the one to tell you the truth."

Damon nodded, bringing himself under control. "It ended up bringing me my wife, so I forgive you."

"I'm glad." Mr. Johnson rose to his feet, rubbing his bald head. "I'll be going, now."

Damon didn't spare him another glance as he left the room, instead focusing on Jeff. "What? Why are you looking at me like that?"

"Just proves the point I've been trying to beat into your thick skull all along. You can't trust everyone who 'works' for you."

Damon sighed. "I know. Believe me, I know. I've been working on being more involved lately. And I shall continue to grow ever more so. Apparently, you can't trust people when it comes to money," he said.

"You think?" Johanna said, meeting his eyes.

His face grew hot and he dropped his own gaze to his hands. "I know. I need to focus more on my personal and business life. I'm trying."

"Yes, you are. But you have a long way to go," Johanna said. "I hope you realize now just how many people out there would love to take advantage of you."

"Oh, come now. There can't be *that* many," he argued.

Jeff and Johanna rolled their eyes.

Damon chuckled. "Okay, okay. I get it. The rich boy learned his lesson. Cue the commercial break."

"Good," Jeff said. Grabbing his jacket, he saluted them and headed to the door. "On that note, I'm out of here. I have no desire to listen to the two of you moaning for the rest of the day."

Johanna closed her eyes, blushing, but Damon only chuckled. "He's right. I plan on making you moan all night."

"Hm. I think I need food first," she replied. "Baby is hungry."

"Well, in that case, follow me. Maybe I'll cook for you, and test out my independent streak a little bit more." He shrugged, rubbing his head. "It can't be that hard, can it?"

"Uh, honey?" She hesitated. "Not on your life. Leave the cooking to the professional, please. Baby likes tasty food, not what you would make."

He scowled at her over his shoulder. "Are you insinuating that I wouldn't make a good cook?"

"Yep. Absolutely."

"Oh ye of little faith." He chuckled. "You have no idea what I can do when I set my mind to it."

She knew exactly what he could do. He'd won her over, after all.

If he could do that, he could do anything.

Epilogue

VALENTINE'S DAY, 2012

Amazing how one year could change a life.

One year ago, Johanna had been bitter, alone, and incapable of trusting anyone — let alone falling in love. Yet now, she thought her heart might burst with the joy that filled her to overflowing.

And all it had taken was an extremely stubborn, and very handsome, British lord.

Damon looked at her, and a smile lit up his face. Tears shone in his eyes as he turned his attention back to their daughter.

Johanna stared into the child's dark blue eyes with wonder. The baby wailed and scrunched her eyes shut, arching her little back and flailing her fists. Tears spilled down Johanna's cheeks, and she dropped her head back against the pillow. "It's a girl."

"Jessica," he whispered. He reached out a finger tentatively, and the baby latched onto it with a tight grip. "Look! She's holding my hand."

Johanna nodded. "She knows her daddy."

"Yes," he said softly, and smiled down at the baby. "Yes, she does."

· · ·

Johanna lay back on the bed. Damon cradled their daughter close and kissed her tiny nose. He headed back toward Johanna and handed her a cup of apple juice. His eyes were warm and shining with pride. "You were fantastic. You're amazing."

She smiled and sipped her juice. "She's perfect."

"Just like her mother," he said. "I love you both."

"I love you, too."

Damon brushed a finger down the tiny infant's cheek tenderly. The baby grunted, turning her head before letting out a loud cry. Damon grinned at her, handing the baby to Johanna. "She has your temper, too."

"Ha ha. Very funny." She lowered her top and guided the baby to her breast. "She's only hungry. You cry when you're hungry, too."

"Indeed." He scooted closer and dropped a kiss on the infant's wispy blond hair. "I don't blame her one little bit for her choice of dinner, either." Damon plucked the blue envelope out of his jacket, holding it between two fingers. "Guess we don't need this anymore."

"You can open it now," she teased. "Go on. Get it out of your system."

He shook his head but opened it. His eyes widened when he read it. He burst into laughter. "Perhaps it's good that we waited."

"Why? What does it say?"

He handed it to her, still laughing too hard to speak. She read it, then started laughing, too. "You see this, Jessica? You're supposed to be a boy!"

"No one told her, apparently." Damon rubbed his eyes. "Okay. I concede. Next time, we won't find out, either."

"Next time?" she echoed, raising a brow. "Who says there will be a next time?"

"Well…there is the issue of an heir. We have to raise one lord in this world who won't be a greedy prig like his father."

"Ah, yes." She nodded solemnly, biting back a grin. "We can't have your good name die out, now can we?"

"Of course not," he agreed and kissed her lightly. "But next time, I get to stay in the bathroom. After witnessing childbirth, I think I can handle it."

She punched his shoulder. "You never give up, do you?"

He kissed her forehead. "Never."

A knock on the door interrupted them, and Damon drew back with a grin. "Ah. I think Lilly's here."

"Come in," Johanna called.

The door crept open, and Lilly peeked through the door. Her light brown hair framed her sweet heart-shaped face. When she saw Jessica, Lilly's huge smile lit up the room. She stepped inside, then stopped. "Is it a boy or a girl?"

Damon embraced his sister, tugging her inside by the hand. "Come in. It's a girl. Her name is Jessica."

"Jessica. Like Mom," Lilly said.

"Yep. Would you like to hold her? She's done nursing."

"Yes." She nodded. "I would love to hold Jessica."

Damon guided Lilly to the chair, then collected Jessica. "Here you go."

Jessica squirmed, let out a sigh, and closed her eyes. "She likes me," Lilly said.

"How could she not?" Damon answered. His eyes glistened with unshed tears.

"I like her, too," Lilly replied.

Damon sat on the ground at Lilly's feet, whispering soft words to Jessica. Johanna's heart warmed.

"Will you come stay with us for a little while? In your room?" Damon asked.

Lilly pursed her lips and her forehead crinkled. "For Jessica. But then I will go home."

Damon shot Johanna an excited grin. "Sounds good," he said.

"Happy Valentine's Day, Jessica," Lilly said, brushing a kiss to the baby's forehead.

Johanna grimaced. "I guess I can't hate Valentine's Day anymore, can I? I met you on the night before Valentine's Day, and gave birth to Jessica on the damn day, as well."

"Nope. You have to love it now." When she scrunched her nose, he laughed.

"Fine." Johanna grinned. "But only if I have you in my bed every Valentine's Day morning."

"I think we can arrange that." His mouth pressed against hers tenderly. "I love you. Always."

"And I you."

Together, they watched Lilly and Jessica. Life couldn't get any better.

It just couldn't.

Acknowledgments

I absolutely must say thanks to Adrien, my awesome editor. Thank you for making this book shine, and for making me laugh through every round of edits. I can't imagine anyone else being able to make me crack up through hours and hours and hours...okay, you get it. And, most of all, thanks for being such a great friend, on top of all of that. Thank you!

To Entangled, and everyone in it, thanks for inviting me in. I love everyone I've gotten to know here, and can't wait to meet even more of you.

Happy Reading!

About the Author

Diane Alberts is a multi-published, bestselling contemporary romance author with Entangled Publishing. She also writes New York Times, USA Today, and Wall Street Journal bestselling new adult books under the name Jen McLaughlin. She's hit the Top 100 lists on Amazon and Barnes and Noble numerous times with numerous titles. She was mentioned in Forbes alongside E. L. James as one of the breakout independent authors to dominate the bestselling lists. Diane is represented by Louise Fury at The Bent Agency.